Bibliografische Information der Deutschen Nationalbibliothek: Die Deutsche Nationalbibliothek verzeichnet diese Publikation in der Deutschen Nationalbibliografie; detaillierte bibliografische Daten sind im Internet über *dnb.dnb.de* abrufbar.

Bibliographic information of the Deutsche Nationalbibliothek: The Deutsche Nationalbibliothek lists this publication in the Deutsche Nationalbibliografie; detailed bibliographic data are available on the Internet at dnb.dnb.de.

Editing:
Andrea Huebener / Thea Bradbury

Translation:
Thea Bradbury

Covertext:
Christoph Zischek

Production and publishing house:
BoD Books on Demand, Norderstedt

ISBN: 9783752884784

Christoph Huebener

The Flight Log

Oh, I have slipped the surly bonds of earth,
And danced the skies on laughter-silvered wings;
Sunwards I've climbed
and joined the tumbling mirth
of sun-split clouds.
And done a hundred things
You have not dreamed of
Wheeled and soared and swung
high in the sunlit silence.
Hovering there I've chased
the shouting wind along
And flung my eager craft
through footless halls o fair...

Up, up
the long delirious burning blue
I've topped the wind-swept heights
with easy grace
Where never lark, or even eagle, flew;
And, while with silent, lifting mind I've trod
The high untresspassed sanctity of space,
put out my hand and touched the face of God

Pilot Officer John Gillespie Magee, Jr.
No. 412 Squadron RCAF
June 1922 – December 1941

Contents

INTENTIONALLY
LEFT
BLANK

Almost nothing in my life has shaped me to the same extent that flying has.

My stories don't focus on dry technical descriptions or impersonal reporting.

Rather, they offer a glimpse of my experiences; of unforgettable events and everything connected with them.

None of these stories are pure imagination; most really did happen as described - more or less.
A few arose from events which I myself experienced, or are dedicated to people I have flown with or who are very

important to me. Any resemblances are therefore intentional. The thing that unifies all these stories is the incredible miracle of flight and the impossible-to-grasp sensations and emotions which accompany it.

It has always moved me deeply, and continues to do so today.

nice flight

Christoph

Oh, one more thing:
This text contains some terms whose meanings may not be immediately apparent. I considered adding footnotes or a glossary, but decided against it on the advice of my editors. If you would like to know the meanings of these (technical) terms, you can look them up in the relevant sources.
Thank you.

For My Father

This story was actually supposed to be called something completely different.

The title was supposed to involve a word like *start* or *beginning*. After all, it's the first story in this book.

But I decided against it after a discussion. It was my father who made this story happen - and it was my father who introduced me to flying, among many other things. So this (true) story is dedicated to him.

It began in the early seventies. I was around eleven years old and the Wall divided the country, enclosing what was then the GDR. My grandparents lived in isolated, island-like Berlin, and we visited them regularly. The simplest way to do so was by plane from Hanover.

Thanks to subsidies, flights back then were cheap - a little over 60 Deutschmarks for a half-hour flight to Berlin-Tempelhof airport on a British Airways Super One-Eleven or a Pan Am 727. These airliners could reach Berlin via three different corridors through the GDR: Hamburg Air Corridor in the north, Bueckeburg Air Corridor in the centre and Frankfurt Air Corridor in the south. Each was 20 miles wide; there was an ADIZ along the border, as well as widespread aerial surveillance. But of course, I knew nothing of all that back then. My mother and brother were flying to Berlin to visit my grandparents that autumn day. Although for some long-forgotten reason I wasn't travelling with them, my father and I still accompanied them to the airport in Hanover. We made our way from the provinces of Ostwestfalen to the capital of Lower Saxony via train and bus. For me, this was more than just an excursion; it was a real sensation. After all, we weren't just visiting a major city, but also a major airport.

I can still picture myself on the bus from the station to the airport: the closer we got, the more excited I became. And my father was no different; he was as curious as I was about anything to do with aviation, and skilfully explained it all to me.

Back then, Langenhagen (the area of the city where the airport was located) didn't have any industrial buildings to block our view of the airfield, and soon, in the distance, behind the high fence, I could make out the air traffic control tower, which in those days still crouched on top of the plain terminal building. Soon after, we left the bus at the parking area and entered the terminal. The air, impregnated with the scent of kerosene, smelt like perfume to me. The ubiquitous howl of the APUs was broken only by the sound of idling turbines from the planes which I assumed must be starting up or coming to rest on the apron behind the concrete barriers that blocked my view. We proceeded to the check-in. There were promotional gifts from the airlines at the counters (I had long been the proud owner of a Pan Am shoulder bag!), along with colourful stickers for the luggage, which vanished into the unfathomable depths of the building on a clattering conveyer belt. We said our goodbyes; my mother and brother went through the glass door behind the counter, and my father and I struck out up endless flights of stairs towards the remote corner of the building where we would gain the lofty heights of the viewing terrace. We stood, freezing, in the cold autumn drizzle, and, a short time later, watched my mother and brother climb the gangway, waving, and vanish into the aircraft. The cabin door closed as if by magic, the gangway was hauled away by a sweet little tractor, and the plane slowly began to move.

I watched it like a hawk. I watched it waiting at the end of the runway, watched as the gleaming white 727 with the light blue logo on its fin vanished into the low grey stratus clouds with an ear-splitting roar of engines and an imposing plume of exhaust fumes.

The return journey awaited us; the weather started to improve a bit. But there was still a little time left to explore the airfield, so my father and I strolled past the battered silver aluminium cargo containers with their colourful stickers, past the dreary parking lot and storage areas, and along a low, equally joyless service building. Our goal: the fence.

Engines thundered promisingly in the background and we soon found a suitable spot near the wide taxiway that linked the two runways. From here, we could see the planes trundling by from up close – at least until, with another roar of engines, they turned and vanished behind the edge of a forest, only to reappear shortly afterwards, accelerating down the runway and finally ascending into the sky with a deafening din.

We watched this spectacle for a little while before strolling along the fence to the GAT. Here, lined up neatly on the apron, were a huge number of sports planes: Piper PA-28s, Cessna 150s and 172s, P-159Ds, Beechcraft Barons... I even remember seeing a Ryan Navion lashed down in the front row.

Near the apron, set into the green chain-link fence - as tall as a person and somewhat the worse for wear - was a locked door that gave access to the airfield. Next to the door, a white metal sign hung on the fence, promising *SIGHTSEEING FLIGHTS* in embossed black letters. Below, one could discover that a thirty-minute excursion in one of the sports planes would set you back 20 Marks, and that those interested should ring at the door.

Of course, the events and impressions of the last few hours had only increased my desire to go flying myself, and now the desire became a burning urge. My eager glances at the apron, the sign, the bell; my beseeching sidelong looks at my father - they were enough for him to grasp, even without words, what it was I wanted.

My father was and remains the best-tempered man I know, and he attempted to explain that we only had enough money for the train ride back to our village. This information failed to halt my desperate pleas. I regret my stubbornness to this day - or then again, perhaps not.

At last, a miracle occurred: as much to his surprise as to mine, my father discovered another five-Mark note in his pocket - enough for both the longed-for flight and the train ride home. In tearing haste, I dashed to the bell, and a few moments later, a tanned old man appeared and informed my smiling father that I was the final passenger he needed to make the flight - there were already two others waiting. I looked on gratefully as my father proffered the necessary fee. Then, the tanned old man - who now revealed himself to be my pilot - ushered me through the door in the chain-link fence.

I still remember clearly my excitement as I was led across the holy ground of the apron to the aircraft. My knees were weak with the restless expectation that we would be taking off at once.

My pilot's target was a C-172. Creamy white and embellished with red stripes, it stood out on the apron in front of the lines of parked aircraft. There were already two passengers in the back of the plane; a father with his daughter.

I expected to sit in the back with them, and was stunned when the tanned old man opened the starboard door of the Cessna and invited me to take the co-pilot's seat.

Dizzy with this unexpected stroke of luck, I clambered awkwardly into the seat. The tanned old man showed me how to fasten the claret-coloured lap belt and closed the door from the outside.

A few minutes later, he was sitting next to me, smiling and taking his sunglasses from the cockpit shelf without looking. With a grin, he offered me a headset. I hauled it over my ears, still a little clumsy. I was almost bursting with pride - the passengers behind me didn't have headsets!

Now, my pilot began to flip switches and press buttons on the Cessna's beige-coloured plastic dashboard, focusing intently. This was all entirely mysterious to me in those days, but I was nonetheless fascinated.

My headset began to hum gently; the propeller in front of me turned loosely a couple of times before the engine caught loudly and the plane's very foundations seemed to shake.

Shocked, I stared at the various lamps, switches and dials in the cockpit as the motor's hum quietened, allowing me to breathe again. I glanced at my pilot, who gave me a grin, a nod and a thumbs-up. He said something incomprehensible into the microphone - I supposed it must be English - and an equally incomprehensible answer crackled back. He pushed a lever into the dashboard, the engine's roar swelled and the plane began to move. I barely had time to absorb everything that was happening around me - me, in my wonderful co-pilot's seat. A truly incredible feeling!

My pilot nudged me and pointed outside. I saw my father standing by the fence; camera in one hand, waving to me with the other. I waved excitedly back.

Finally, the aircraft turned and left my father in its slipstream. Spellbound, I stared out of the shuddering window at the taxiway sliding slowly away beneath us as we followed its bends and signposted turnings to the runway. We waited, the engine idling impatiently. After a few minutes and some more gibberish from the radio, my pilot took the plane's brakes off again, let it roll onto a kind of oversized zebra crossing, turned it to the left and lined it up with the runway. Before us lay two kilometres of concrete, inconceivably wide; sunlight shimmered through the clouds at the end of the strip.

I looked over at my pilot, a little nervous. He gave me a nod, opened the throttle, and then stared by turns at the instruments and straight ahead through the cockpit window, in deep concentration.

The Cessna accelerated smoothly; the runway slipped away beneath us faster and faster; finally, I heard his voice through the headset - *Look out* - and, with one smooth movement of the yoke, the plane lifted off from the ground and we rose gently into the sky over Hanover. I looked down, and it was as though the whole world belonged to me alone. The edge of the airfield slipped away beneath us, the forest shrank and, in the distance, lakes sparkled tentatively in the sun. We made a gentle curve to the left and Hanover shimmered before us in silhouette. The clouds had broken up and we climbed slightly, approaching one of the gaps. The engine thrummed, warm and powerful, the sun peeked dazzlingly through the scattered clouds and we circled giddily above the world, city and country. I couldn't get enough of the view; my heart turned somersaults of delight and I felt as though this whole miraculous world of sunlight, cockpit, patchy clouds and toybox landscape below had been created just for me.

I was beside myself when my pilot indicated that I should put both hands on the yoke in front of me. I couldn't quite believe it when I felt the cool black plastic under my small fingers. I quickly understood the motions that he entered and which the aircraft followed.

What more can I tell you?

We circled Hanover, and this half hour in the clouds felt to me like an entire lifetime; the slow descent that quickly brought the airport into view before us again, the purring landing at the edge of the vast runway, the engine still running. I still remember the slight floating sensation during the descent and the gentle thump when we reached the ground; the mischievous expression on my pilot's face; my fingers still carefully clutching the yoke; the engine shuddering in the airframe - I felt as though I was the very first pilot in history.

Finally, the creamy-white Cessna with its red stripes trundled off the vast runway and onto the taxiway, whose curves and signposts we followed back to the apron with its dozens of sports planes sitting motionless in the distance.

Now, at last, we swung back into our own parking spot; the engine died away and the plane shook once again. My pilot laid his sunglasses back on the shelf without looking, took my headset back and - very professionally, I felt - undid the claret-coloured lap belt with the big buckle himself.

My father - who I now realise was hugely relieved - stood behind the chain-link fence, waving at me. Calm and unshaken, I raised my hand in answer.

Then the starboard door snapped open and I hopped out onto the concrete, bursting with confidence. My pilot, tanned and laughing, shook my hand; I'm sure he gave me some kind of compliment as well.

I raced over to my father, who folded me into his arms. During the late afternoon train ride home, I alternated between silence and floods of words. It's only today that I understand how profoundly the experience shaped me - it was unforgettable.

My father - who had been interested in aviation all his life yet never quite got as far as flying himself - gave me an experience that showed me where I belonged and that led to nearly thirty almost indescribable years as a pilot.

My confirmation present was the glider lessons that I'd been longing for. To my parent's chagrin, however, I spent far more time on the airfield than I did in school - a fact which eventually came to light despite my elaborate attempts to cover it up.

My glider lesson funding abruptly dried up. The consequences were appalling: I endured my academic nosedive stoically and without much concern, but having to look up at the sky and see others flying without me was almost unendurable.

When I started to earn money through my apprenticeships and the numerous jobs that I took during my studies, I invested almost all of it in flying, spending many, many hours soaring above the world and gathering incredible experiences.

Incidentally, I was later able to take my father with me on numerous impressive flights - but they'll never repay what I owe him.

These Evenings

It's time for the final flights of the year. The weather is getting rapidly worse and sometimes we end up flying through squadrons of showers, beneath low-hanging clouds, trying to climb through the rare gaps in the grey ceiling to enjoy the sun above, low as it already is. Warm light blazes through the plexiglas of our aircraft canopies. But the rough wind robs us of the poignant calm of gliding: flying in these angry airstreams is more like a furious car race over an unpredictable stretch of potholes. Hard thrusts of the rudder, tightly-fastened safety belts, showers of rain concealing the view, strong sidewinds turning landings into complex feats of acrobatics.

At some point, this will all be over as well.

In the never-ending autumn rain, the airfield is transformed into a sodden pasture which dooms even the simplest attempt at taxiing. The hall doors rattle in the wind; the airfield becomes desolate: no more hustle and bustle of planes taxiing back and forth, taking off and landing; no more roar of engines.

All abandoned and alone.

Many of our planes now stand, covered, in the dimly lit, damp, draughty hangar. Some of them have been dismembered into skeletal components; a few have even been robbed of their wings. Their colourful, grubby cable entrails spill from their covered engine hoods as though from open wounds. There are oily tools everywhere; trestles and tables with discarded parts; above the workbenches are tacked crumpled plans, lists, exploded diagrams soiled with oily fingerprints. Along the walls stand chaotic shelves stacked with spare parts: generators, dusty crates and boxes labelled with beige dockets dangling from thin cords. Rusty petrol cans in an unlit corner; scrap stacked on top of them. A row of battered military lockers, resting place of all manner of documents.

Above hang individual ribs, disassembled ailerons and a complete vertical stabiliser. Enamel signs advertising aircraft manufacturers, discoloured aerial photos in crooked frames, portraits of this pilot or other; a gritty residue of dust, oil and dirt on the sloping ledges. Beneath the roof, out of harm's way, hangs the gutted steel airframe of a Piper Cub. Lid-shaped tin lampshades dangle from long cables, swaying with every gust of wind and setting delicate traceries of shadow dancing on the ground.

Yet even here, we have our rituals. Gently, almost lovingly, we stroke the shapely shells of our planes as we walk past: smooth, cool tin paneling, snug coverings, plastic fairings polished to a shine and soft cotton moulding gently to the shape of the machine below. It's as though we're afraid of losing touch with these sleeping birds of ours.

We meet here almost every weekend. As soon as we can - often in the early afternoon on Fridays - we flee the work week for this hangar. We cram ourselves into unflattering overalls, our pockets overflowing with oily rags, remnants of gloves and other little tools, and clean every inch of our planes with the utmost care. We swap out parts, twist ourselves into knots and almost stand on our heads to tinker with the instruments in narrow cockpits, bend over huge clamps to sand and file things, repair, with oil-smeared faces, motors mounted on special trestles, change gaskets, lay steering cables, change lights and tires, solder cable harnesses, redo paintwork, polish and clean. We talk very little. Now and again, a tool clatters to the chilly concrete floor amid curses; a radio drones steadily away in a corner; the coffee machine in the corner chortles regularly to itself; and the work lamps continue to throw their jittering shadows across the walls of the hall. Outside, it has long since grown dark. Enough for today.

We linger listlessly for a while among the slumbering aircraft, as though unable to part from them. Tidying. We find these evenings long now. They're somehow different to those in summer. More predictable.

But we don't talk about that.

Finally, we wad up our work things and wrap our beloved flight jackets around our shoulders. Lights out. Locking up. Out.

Then, at last, we drive our old cars a few kilometres through the rainy darkness to the nearby village. We have a pub there. Much too loud. Cramped and smoky. Always crowded. Standing room only, oppressive closeness, dim lighting, videoclips thundering down at us from the monitors. Unbearable, really.

But we always go there.

So we slam the car doors closed behind us and run through the interminable rain to the sanctuary of the pub. A torrent of music, laughter and confused voices pours out at us through the cigarette smoke when we open the door. We force our way through the frankly unbelievable crowd to the back corner of the room and cluster around a tiny table. It's like this place was made for us. Despite everything. Where else could we tipsily take up residence in our self-imposed cliches? On these evenings.

Compensation.

But we don't take any notice of that.

It doesn't take long for the first glints of mischief to appear in our eyes. The inevitable pools of beer around the ashtray, the bluff backslapping to welcome late arrivals, the adventurers' cigarettes in the sleeve pockets of our flight jackets.

In accordance with our status, we favour garishly coloured, high-proof drinks of indefinable composition. Blocky naphtha lighters flare briefly; we suck silently at straws and cigarettes. The din in the room doesn't really allow for conversation; instead, we yell clipped sentences at each other and exchange meaningful glances. An overture of sorts. Introverted daredevils with unreadable expressions, sworn to solidarity. Better than any film.

Some time later, right on schedule, someone gives the first cue; the introduction to the already familiar *do-you-remember-when* stories. Loud laughter booms from our corner; we draw closer together, the better to shout at each other. A slim girl advances laboriously towards us with a huge tray and replaces the empty glasses with an acrobatic movement. But we're already luxuriating in the memories of past flights, an astonishingly systematic stack of them. Images. After all, we're not just *any old pilots*.

Wild laughter; we bask in unbelievable stories, the alcohol transforms little rainclouds into an impenetrable storm front, muscular narratives of gust fronts, failing electronics, stuttering engines, ice build-up. A shake of the head. No escape. Impossible.

Cold sweat is clearly visible on the eloquent narrator's forehead. Still, he managed it somehow. Obviously more luck than anything else.

Second round: off-field landing in a glider. Last year.

Really. No, really.

No airfield to be seen anywhere, just never-ending forest. Spotting the clearing at - of course - the oft-cited very last second. About the size of a hand towel and totally covered in scrub, but the only possible option. The only one.

Tailwind landing, obviously. The pilot still doesn't know how he did it: not a single scratch on the machine.

He can still hear the rustling of the treetops against the tail just before the landing. Unforgettable. And we don't show any weakness: approving nods.

We're slowly winding up to the height of our powers.

Endless breakbeats pound mercilessly down at us from the speakers; someone's illustrative arm movement knocks a full glass of beer over the table, to the accompaniment of hoots from the others; confused swearing.

We still have a couple more variants to offer.

Do-you-know-the-guy-who.

Increasingly implausible, bloodcurdling stories:

Student pilots doing loops around high-voltage power lines; emergency deadstick landings with a cold engine on bustling motorways; mechanics accidentally shooting themselves through the hangar roof on ejector seats. Close encounters of the third kind - near misses with low-flying jets.

Locking eyes with an A-10 pilot.

The crowd has got thicker.

We spy a few good-looking girls in the corner opposite. Man, if only they knew. But nobody says it.

Overflowing ashtrays.

After some hemming and hawing, we wave the girls in the corner over to us; they push their way through the crowd towards us, giggling. One pretty dark-haired one with huge eyes, one dolled-up, posh-looking blonde.

The other two plainer: wallflowers. Furtive glances. *What's-your-name-what-are-you-up-to*.

Clowning around. More drinks.

We're as reticent as ever, following the established script.

We act polite, interested. If we mention the fact that we all fly, we only do so in occasional, carefully calculated asides. We know how this goes. Stay cool, understated, weigh each sentence. The blonde immediately enters into the pantomime, presents herself as worldly-wise, develops a sudden interest in joining us.

Anyway.

The evening suddenly seems to be over. Nothing's happening.

We return to sucking on our cigarettes and our drink straws.

One of the wallflowers really does have to go home now.

But we still want to do something else.

We discuss various ideas, but that's as far as we get. Nothing that's acceptable to everyone.

After a long interval of lazing around, someone remembers that the nth rerun of *Top Gun* is playing this evening at a nearby provincial cinema.

We're abruptly wide awake again; the girl with the huge tray has her work cut out for her figuring out what everyone owes; and of course someone hasn't brought enough change and it takes forever for us to force our way back through the crush to the door.

We just want to get away from here.

Finally, we run through the ongoing rain to our cars; the remaining girls climbing in behind us.

We fling ourselves into the seats, soaking wet, slam the doors and race - far too fast - to the little hamlet with the cinema.

The girls enjoy it.

The word *RESIDENZ* blazes above the little cinema in yellow neon. The 'i' is faulty and flickering. The ticket seller is astonished by this unaccustomed late-night rush; she unearths the last ten cans of beer from her little bar.

Besides us, there are just two dark shapes in the front rows. We suddenly realise that one of our lot is missing. And the blonde is gone too.

He's going to have a story to tell tomorrow.

The dismal little screen's tatty plush curtain draws aside immediately and our beer cans hiss open.

We accompany the familiar adverts with mocking commentaries as loud as they are impatient.

It's only when the first jets crash down onto the flight deck to the accompaniment of Harold Faltermeier's music that we settle down to enjoy the opening credits, attempting to decipher the idiosyncratic ballet of the deck crew.

We crane our necks, review the aerial manoeuvres critically and expertly, bawl out the songs.

During the (in our opinion entirely unnecessary) love scenes, we discuss particularly successful manoeuvres in an undertone. We're beside ourselves over the more hazardous stunts. Our eyes gleaming, we slide down further in our seats - right hand on the stick, left hand on the throttle - incredible!

As the last F-14 vanishes into the orange-red evening sky behind the closing credits and the lights come up, dazzling, in the auditorium, we haul ourselves wearily from our seats and trail through the wind and rain to our cars.

As always on these evenings, the hard core of our group ends up in the pub again. It's long since emptied out: a few couples sit by themselves at the tables; the music is significantly quieter.

The girl with the huge tray smiles when we order coffee.

Our silence is no longer feigned; our conversations are quieter, more sentimental, remembrances:
our formation flight above the clouds at sunset with the three Cubs, and the subsequent landing in the last light on the stunning, solitary plateau that wasn't really an airfield at all.
The time we landed the Speed Canard almost on the beach of the lonely swimming island in Sweden: out of the cockpit and into the water.
East over the Alps with the 172 six ship to Balaton.
The drinking bout that followed the off-field landing with the glider on that French farm two years ago.
And the time we christened our new Mooney with champagne and it ended up getting into the ventilation system so that the boxes in the cockpit still smell sweet today.

Quiet laughter; the hundreds of stories of our past exploits that we use to get ourselves through the dullness of the working week.

And of the adventures that we still hope to have.

It's long gone midnight; we sit silently around the table, each of us lost in our own thoughts and dreams.
Then we discover that we're the last people left in the pub.

The little waitress begins to stack the chairs on the tables:
almost like we're in a film, we think.
Finally, she brings us another coffee on the house and sits down
at our table to settle up and to chat with us.

Not long after, we slap each other wearily on the back once
again, over our flight jackets; a wistful farewell ritual.

Until next weekend.

The Blue Hour

They'd always thought we were pretty mad. Of course, we enjoyed our reputation - and cultivated it assiduously.

I can't remember who came up with this crazy idea, but to be honest, it doesn't really matter any more.
We just started doing it at some point, and since then we've done it every year.
It's almost a spring tradition.
As if to say,
Look – it's happening. Now. Finally!
When my alarm clock startles me awake at two thirty in the morning, I'm still much too tired to bother rationally analysing

what I'm doing. I just get up instead.

Obviously everything is still pitch black outside, and when I stumble through the nocturnal kitchen to the fridge, I remember that we were planning to have breakfast at the airfield. I slam the door again sullenly.

Growling stomach, parched throat: a gulp of orange juice, at least. Rushing through the bathroom, fishing my flight jacket from the wardrobe. My worn helmet bag with its headset and other essential tools is ready to go. Always.

Keys. And we're off.

I'm sure my neighbours are delighted by my messing around loudly with the garage door first thing on a Sunday morning, as well as the streak I tear through the silent estate shortly afterward, tyres howling. Almost no cars on the road; streetlights dark; quiet, gentle music on the radio; I'm still not quite fully awake.

A good thing my subconscious knows the way to the airfield. The cold motor toils reluctantly. We're outside the town now. The night seems to be darker here, no sign of life, unreal. The gate is open. The narrow track that leads to the hangars. The switchback ride over the innumerable potholes slowly dispels my fatigue.

I stop in front of our log cabin. Nobody here yet.

Bloody freezing outside; I'm glad I've got my warm flight jacket.

Never noticed before how quiet it is here at night.

I stand alone in the damp night air in front of the hangar for a reverent moment, and breathe deeply.

The lonely world around me.

Opening up the cabin; turning on the lights, heating and coffee machine. I sit at the big table, staring through the window at the dark airfield. Silence.

Soon, a pair of spotlights appears in the distance. I go outside again, forced to shield my dazzled eyes with my hand as the car bears down on me. The others trundle in slowly, loaded with breakfast things, maps, kneeboards, headphones. We strew it all in a jumble on the table and wait in silence until the coffee finally takes effect - a downright uncommunicative group sitting unshaven around the table, clutching coffee mugs, picking drowsily at various pastries.

It's obvious that nobody really wanted to get up. I rummage in my sleeve pocket for cigarettes.

At last, with an effort, we set ourselves in motion: looking through the cupboards for our things, shooting the first concerned glances at the time. We haven't got long now. We stumble into the hangar through the little side door. In the darkness, it seems to go on forever. Finally, the neon tubes flare, diffusing a punishingly artificial greenish light. A switch sets the electric motor's relays clicking and the rusty hangar door judders and whines slowly upwards; clammy air streams in.

We haul the covers from the wings and bodies of the planes and push them out into the dark of the night. Everything still silent. Hardly a word.

Preflight check with a torch: I prowl around our 337, run my hands over the propeller and the leading edges of the wings, move the rudder, open maintenance flaps, shine my light into narrow openings, check the time repeatedly as I go.

Our flight controller isn't here yet, either. Shit. We even called him yesterday.

Hopefully he'll turn up.

The second hand races impassively around our big pilots' watches. Half an hour left.

Damn it.

The planes' plexiglass windows are already fogged up; my Chucks are sopping from the dew on the ankle-deep airfield grass. Then, in the distance, another pair of lights stab through the ground fog, approaching the airfield. A little later, we hear the steel door of the tower click shut, warm light flares in the hall windows, and within minutes, the rotating light on the tower starts to move.

I've checked the oil level; I spin the prop a couple more times. Same procedure for the rear engine. The others are standing on the wings of their machines in the clammy darkness; I can see them waving in silhouette.

Now. It's happening.

Finally.

I wave back, clap my copilot on the shoulder and open the door to the Cessna. Slide into the dark cockpit, pull the door shut. Maps clipped in front, under the window; kneeboard on the right leg; thermos behind; I feel for the ignition key; click the master switch; the gyros begin to hum. The switch to illuminate the control panel is somewhere around here. After some groping around, we find it; the red light from the instruments makes things easier.

Headset on. Startup clearance?

The flight controller's exhaustion is clear from his mumble.

We grin at each other: he thinks we're completely nuts.

But at least he made it.

We slowly get underway; find our words again; familiar

movements in the cockpit; first grins; our mood improves, further dispelling the tiredness. ACL, position lights, avionics off, ignition key turned, and after a couple of laborious cranks, the front engine coughs into life. The rear one follows suit. The propeller wash forces thin trickles of condensed fog slowly across the front window. We're still frozen stiff; the heating in the cockpit is impossibly slow to get started.

I look over at the other aircraft. The engines are running. I release the brakes, open the throttle slightly and start taxiing across the field to the starting position. The jittering cone of the taxi light. The cabin isn't really warming up.

The Mooney is in front of me, the strobe lights at the ends of the wings flashing through the thick black air. Someone seems to have jammed my engines' temperature gauges at zero; the needles are barely moving. Five minutes to go.

Avionics on, quick radio check; the others answer on our frequency. I tune into the tower frequency: *Earlybird formation, line up two-six and wait*, crackles the flight controller in our headsets.

Throttle a little wider; we taxi very slowly onto the runway. It's all going as discussed, planned, briefed.

Four aircraft in fingertip formation: the Mooney up ahead on the centerline as number one, me a plane's length to the right and behind as number two, behind and to my left the Beech as number three, and to the right of it the Turbo Arrow.

The planes stand, roaring, on the jet-black runway. It ends in a black sky: no horizon in sight.

Two minutes to go.

Take-off checks. We go through the familiar routine.

A crackle through the headset: *Number one is ready.* I press the talk button: *Two ready.*

Three ready, brief pause, *four ready.*

Frequency change. More crackling: *Tower, Earlybird formation ready.*

Roger, QHN 998, Earlybird formation is cleared take-off two-six, wind is calm.

Our lead repeats the clearance. Crackling.

Frequency change.

I watch the onboard clock's second hand: twenty seconds left. I put the brakes on, take-off power setting, glance out of the window; the other aircraft are also trembling with suppressed energy on the wet runway.

Release breakes............. now.

The second hand hits twelve as our aircraft begin to move: five fifteen precisely.

Sunrise.

We spread out wide in formation as we leave the traffic circuit. Far behind us at the edge of the clouds is the first almost invisible pale azure stripe, only barely brighter than the deep blue of the night surrounding us; I orient myself by the Mooney's starboard light and follow it into the shallow curve. We climb higher; the first shreds of dark grey cloud flit past our aircraft; another gentle curve to the left; and then, at last, we're above the clouds and I squeeze my eyes shut, dazzled; it's already so bright up here.

The sun, a vast, blazing orange-red ball, is crawling ever so slowly above the clouds on the horizon to the east. The clouds a

hazy black mass below us; the gleaming silhouette of the
Mooney in front of me; the other planes staggered behind us,
wings swaying gently; shimmering, glittering swoops of the
propeller in the first light of day above an endless, impossibly
coloured plain of clouds.
I breathe in deeply, suddenly well-nigh overwhelmed, and could
almost yell with joy.
I look to my left; the lads in the Beech wave at us; I pass the
gesture on; my copilot slaps his thigh like a child and beams at
me.

We fly at low altitude, speeding just above the blanket of cloud;
giving ourselves over to this ecstatic dream, these impossible
colours, the speed and the stunning beauty of the dawn sky. The
sun rises ever higher; its light altering the magnificent play of
colours almost from minute to minute. The indistinct grey fades
from the blanket of cloud below us and it begins to take on
colour, looking as light as thistledown.

My copilot has taken over from me and I dig the thermos out
from behind my seat, pour hot coffee into the plastic beaker and
lean back, at ease.
The formation drones cosily through the sky, still widely spaced.

I know that we're all alone with our thoughts now. That no-one
will say another word.
That each of us is staring through his windscreen as though it
were his first time up here. Above the clouds. In the sun. That
our thoughts are abruptly where they belong. That our senses
have suddenly expanded.

Absorbing all the unique, unrepeatable beauty of this early flight. Like a prayer, I think briefly.

And I'm reminded of the words of Richard Bach, who once said that at some point, everybody who flies has to pay their debt for this experience, has to pass on what they've witnessed. And I realise once again what a gift it is to fly up here.

The sun is blindingly bright by now; I can its reflection glinting from the planes up ahead. I switch off the control panel lights; we slowly change course; the formation draws easily and cleanly together. I know what's coming now: the return flight is always the same.

Our adrenalin starts to pump.

We slowly descend onto the colourful carpet of cloud, pull our seatbelts a little tighter, push the throttle open a few more millimetres and close the ranks of our formation even further. Gazes locked on the wings of the pilot in front, we draw closer together, almost touching, and race with incredible speed over the surface of the clouds, riding every wave.

Cloudsurfing.

The kick. The pure thrill of speed.

The lead plane tilts gently to the side to change course again, the ADF needle pivots in the direction of our flight path. We're flying towards our NDB; soon we'll be above the airfield again.

We're still skimming just above the cloud layer - now grey once more - low and furiously fast, waiting tensely for the signal.

The pièce de résistance; the same every year.

The headset crackles and we know that it's the lead aircraft reporting in: *Standby for countdown, acknowledge.*

There's an intent pause once everyone has spat their *Check!* into the microphone.

We're all glancing at our instruments, at the airspace.

Steady, steady…

Split off – three, two, one .…now!

In a flash, I pull the yoke towards me and the Cessy shoots up like a rocket. Below me, I can see the other aircraft scattering, as though the formation has been struck by lightning. My altimeter whirls like a clock; yelling, I turn the plane on its side; overbanking in a turn, we climb higher and higher; just a little more bank for a feint at a downturn; we dive, I bring the aircraft gently back under control, the speed indicator deep into the yellow… and a few minutes later, we're chasing each other riotously: throttles wide open, needles spinning off the dials, playing together, chasing each other, overtaking, circling, diving and shooting up again into this bright, miraculously blue sky.

And then the formation assembles once again.

Piece by piece.

Until everyone is back in position.

At last, we're flying just above the clouds again. We spread out for a shallow descent through the first wisps.

A grey wall, growing ever darker and drearier.

Returning to another world.

Gloom beneath the clouds. It's pouring with rain when we announce our approach: *Earlybird formation in one thousand, three minutes out, for landing.*

Wo kommt ihr denn her? asks the controller, deliberately bored, not bothering with the standard pilot's English. *Where did you lot come from, then?*

From above, answers a dry, sonorous voice, and I have to smile.

The First Flight

A silhouette, he thought. The windsock stood out sharply against the mild red horizon of the evening sky. Above soared a vault of deep blue. He could see her standing there, motionless, leaning against the windsock's mast, head lowered. Her long hair hung around her face, concealing her profile.

For a long time, he simply stood there, motionless, leaning against the cold metal of the hangar door, hands deep in the pockets of his flight jacket. He drank in the image one last time, and realised suddenly that it no longer caused him pain. He shook his head and laughed quietly, then turned away and went slowly over to where his Bellanca Scout stood in the billowing grass. Sat down on the wheels, put his head in his hands and stared at the evening sky.

The engine block ticked gently.

All over.

Quite suddenly, like an unexpected shower of rain. They had thought they knew each other. Or at least, he had thought so. He should have sensed it, he saw that now. Much earlier. He didn't understand why she had left. She'd suddenly rejected him. Just like that. No argument preceding it; nothing. No rational reason. He wasn't prepared; he didn't understand anything anymore. But then the shock hit him sharply and he woke up again. He began to look for solutions, to make plans, to observe and interpret, to consider everything carefully. Over and over. But it had no effect. Pointless.

He didn't see his error. Taking totally the wrong approach, he began to ignore what made her unique. As though he were blind, like before.

He felt misunderstood. He focused only on himself, came to his own defence. Tried everything. Everything.

The long discussions of bygone evenings, crowded with sorrow, jealousy and pain. Endless telephone conversations, letters. Self-righteous panaceas.

She didn't seem to understand at all, spurned him ever more

systematically, was soon avoiding every attempt to explain. He couldn't make sense of it, couldn't explain himself any further, felt totally lost.

And things continued to get worse.

She withdrew further, evading him.

He didn't recognise her anymore.

With every encounter, she became more silent, more unreachable. It seemed to him that she was no longer listening to anyone except herself. He had the impression that she was simply going to drop everything.

Without cause.

Falling into a void.

And then contact broke off for good.

But he didn't give up. He couldn't.

Out of desperation at his own loneliness, really; he understood that now.

He talked with his friends, sought help, but it didn't get him any further: glib maxims, well-intentioned advice, pity, pretty words that meant nothing. They didn't accept his decisions; had no answer to his hopes and desires. Inane assessments of the situation. Pity. He felt abandoned.

Then he discovered ways of distracting himself: parties, booze-ups at other airfields, weekend excursions to visit old friends; things he didn't seem to have done for ages.

But her image kept reeling him in against his will, memories reared up before his eyes and his loneliness only became more complete.

He hesitated for a long, long time, and it was the last attempt

that he allowed himself. Night after night of muddled dreams.
He prepared himself slowly and very carefully for it, hellishly
afraid. He sat in front of the telephone for a long time,
weighing up words, laying out questions and answers, again and
again. He thought it all through one final time; his fingers
trembled as he dialled her number.
A few words. Almost trivial.
Her acquiescence sounded indifferent, and yet he clutched at it
in order to preserve his last hope.
And yet in fact he understood what was happening and chose
to continue deceiving himself.

He had wanted to go flying with her one last time in the absurd
hope that he'd be able to get through to her once again.
His heart raced as it had at their first meeting when he stood
outside her door with the car and honked to pick her up. Much
too early. His tension almost robbed him of the last of his
strength; he saw her leaving the door; brown suede jacket,
maroon jeans, her long hair. How else, he thought, and
struggled simply to sit there.
Uncertain greeting, uneasy glances. Not a word during the
journey to the airfield.
So natural, he thought, while she helped get the Bellanca ready
for takeoff with familiar movements.
Like it used to be…
The engine began to roar; he turned halfway around; saw her
sliding the headset over her long hair; turned the intercom on
and heard her breathing through his headphones.
He set the flaps, smoothly opened the throttle; the plane leapt
above the circle of grass and lifted away.

Flaps, ascent, RPM, climb performance. His hands moved mechanically.

He wasn't really there in the plane; his body was carrying out the familiar movements on its own.

Soon, they reached the bottom of the loose layer of cumulus clouds; ascended through the first wisps into the radiant blue. Level off.

Are you still there, he said, with real effort.

Yes, she replied, almost inaudibly. Her voice sounded grave, occupied. Infinitely sad.

He squinted into the glaring sun; turned the plane around.

It's so beautiful up here, he heard her say quietly through the headphones, and his sadness only grew. Deep and painful.

He steered the plane around the towers of cloud as though sleepwalking; fighting his tears and his memories of the past; trying to fathom her thoughts and yet not succeeding.

Why couldn't he feel what was happening inside her?

Questions. He felt overwhelmed.

The Bellanca droned sonorously above the blanket of cloud; the needles of the instruments vibrated.

Before, they had sped through the sky with the exuberance of children. Everything was so natural; her nonchalance had always impressed him.

How easy things can be, he thought.

As he turned the plane gently on its side for a change of course, he turned around again; saw her sitting behind him. She was staring up into the sky, head propped in her hands, hair dishevelled; she had taken the headset off, it dangled uselessly from a strut. He saw her eyes gleaming; he saw the tears running silently down her gentle face in the roar of the engines, and he turned away, caught in the act.

Then, with a start, he recognised his limitations.
It was as though a weight had fallen from him.
Almost spontaneously, he slowly began to feel calmer.
He parted ways with everything: his fear, his egotism, his self-deceit, his grief.

And he parted ways with her.

He concentrated on the plane again, felt its movements, looked out at the horizon and the endless carpet of cloud; he sensed his freedom once more.
And now he sensed her freedom too; he recognised the cage that he had trapped her in; he saw her loneliness and her immense vulnerability.

He had done it.

He manoeuvered the Scout very gently through the sky, beginning the descent. Soon, the little plane disappeared down through a gap in the clouds.
A little later, it landed on the grass runway and taxied to a standstill. The engine gave one last roar; the propeller spun uselessly; a clattering sound.
He opened the cabin door, got out and helped her out of the plane.

I want to walk a bit, she said, without looking at him, and he nodded.

He watched her as she walked over to the windsock; kept watching.

I've lost her, he thought.

Cat Bravo Yankee

I still can't believe this story. Can't believe it because it's a story in which, as a result of a number of connected events, something suddenly materialises.

It's the kind of incident that everyone is familiar with from films and books. After you've seen it or read it, you often think, nice film. Or, nice book. But it's fictional.

It wouldn't really happen.

And yet.

My story begins in the summer of 1973. I was about thirteen and, together with my parents and my younger brother, was taking the train to the Baltic coast for a few weeks' holiday, just as we'd done the previous year. To be precise, we were on our way to the Bay of Lübeck; to Scharbeutz, located almost exactly at the centre of the bay.

Seat reservations in hand, we shared tea, sandwiches and fruit as we headed north. When we reached Lübeck, we changed to a little regional train which, some time later, deposited us in a small town by the sea.

My parents had rented a tiny apartment in the basement of a holiday home somewhere on Scharbeutz's southern outskirts, with a kitchen and all the trimmings.

To reach the beach, we followed the road through the town. There we found our beach chair with its obligatory sandcastle among a crowd of countless other beach chairs with their obligatory sandcastles.

On warm days, armed with a rubber dinghy, we could spend hours out on the water. There was a pier where tourist steamers made regular stops, and from time to time, we crossed beneath it in the dinghy. Manoeuvring between the mussel-encrusted pillars was no mean feat in the - to our minds, considerable - swell.

At times, depending on the direction of the wind, vast numbers of jellyfish, which we employed as missiles, washed up; our parents' friends visited, bringing with them lovestruck daughters of no interest to me; and there were various walks along the beach to Haffkrug or even to Timmendorfer Strand. Otherwise, it was a thoroughly dull place.

However, there was one highlight: the navy open day, when a destroyer or a frigate anchored in the roads of the bay and a dinghy shuttled curious visitors on board. Personally, I was much more interested in the naval pilots' H-34s helicopter, which were in the habit of landing between the beach road and the dunes with a thunderous roar and could then be inspected as well. Preferably by me.

Preferably every day.

When the weather was bad, the town offered the typical dreary seaside attractions: meals at the popular fish restaurant and at the milk bar on the beach road; creating garish pop art pictures at the little shop where you could spray acrylic paint onto a piece of paper rotating in a tank.

And there was a cinema.

I often stood in front of the glass cases, looking at the film posters. Any day now, a new film would be released: ... *All the Way, Boys!*

Behind what I then still considered to be a pretty impressive title lay one of Terence Hill and Bud Spencer's slapstick comedies, which back then were being churned out more or less every six months.

But the photos in the case nonetheless attracted my attention: aeroplanes! It had aeroplanes in it!

The weather was bad, so it wasn't difficult to beg the necessary cinema money from my parents. I headed down the beach promenade towards the cinema in the drizzle, and a few hours later, I was sitting excitedly in the matinee.

The plot is straightforward: Plata and Salud are small-time crooks who *crash-land* old planes in the South American jungle as part of an insurance fraud scheme run by Salud's perpetually drunken brother.

Eventually they set up a company supplying prospectors and fly their provisions to a high plateau in a clapped-out hippie Boeing Stearman. An aging prospector, an antagonist and a gem mine then cause various complications. And fights. So far, so good.

I was impressed right from the opening sequence, when the pink Dakota swooped over the jungle with its starboard engine on fire before pulling off a thoroughly unorthodox landing at the busy Rio de Janeiro airport, diving into a hangar almost without braking, destroying a T-33 and finally coming to a smouldering halt.

The pilots were impossibly smooth customers, leaving the hangar under the Dak's flipped-down elevator, trading super-cool quips in their beaten-up clothes.

And then: the Catalina.

I fell in love with the PBY in the moment Terence Hill parked his Harley on the apron and raced around the flying boat in his reflective pilot's glasses.

I also fell in love with it in the moment when the Cat roared down the runway and rose into the air, the landing gear vanishing sluggishly into its bay. The few aerial views taken between Macapá and Santarém, a couple of shots from the cockpit, the crash-landing in the jungle clearing - I was blown away by it all.

How incredible it must feel to fly such a huge plane; one that could even land on water. What a wonderful machine!

The film ran its course and I trudged my way through the plot. As the slapstick story wore on, it also featured the ineptly painted Stearman, a Beaver, a geriatric Cessna 150A and an HS 748, but it was the Catalina that impressed me the most.

The holiday came to an end and we returned to the provinces of Lower Saxony. Back at home, I quickly discovered that the film was still playing at our town's *Regina* cinema, and so, soon enough, I was back in front of the screen, watching the PBY thundering into the South American skies once again.

What wouldn't I have given to fly that plane, just once! But it was impossible: it was an old plane from the time of the war, which - if it still existed anywhere -- certainly wouldn't be found in Germany. And if it were? How would I even get close to it, let alone take a flight?

How?

It might sound theatrical, but something had grown inside me; something that linked me almost longingly with these old planes. For as long as I could remember, they had exerted an immense fascination over me - I was deeply impressed by the miracle of these huge, old aeroplanes.

And I often dreamed myself into those scenarios...

My new talisman was a leather thong with a bottle opener on it that I wore around my neck, just like Plata in the film.

I often saw myself sitting in the Cat's cockpit; above and a little way behind the cabin thundered the massive radial engines, propellers spinning in silver circles. I clutched the throttle on the overhead panel tightly with my right hand.

A dream. My dream.

The years went by.

First, they brought my wretched school career and the associated early end to my glider training.

But I never forgot the Cat.

I retook my school leaving certificate, did apprenticeships, finally took the qualifications for university entrance, returned to the glider airfield to start flying again.

And that's where I met Bill. Bill was a tug pilot who also flew C-160s at the neighbouring NATO airfield. He was an absolute nutcase - in a good way.

He had been chucked out of the officers' dorm at the base because he'd repaired parts of his Boeing Stearman's massive radial engines in the living area and left huge oil stains on the carpet. As a result, he'd ended up squatting under a tarp with his Stearman in the base's hangar. It didn't do his reputation any damage: if ever anyone was a truly excellent pilot - and with any plane out there, as well - it was Bill. He wasn't just any old madman; he was the madman. A role model. Seriously.

I still remember my towplane exam as a student glider pilot: it was autumn and the weather was truly miserable, with what had to be more than 15 knots of crosswind coming in gusts, but Bill simply said, *Just stay behind me. I'll look out for you.*
So I fooled around in the old, bucking KA-7, concentrating furiously, the flying teacher cursing loudly behind me, the rudders constantly under attack by the unexpectedly ugly eddies on the lee side of our local hill, attempting to keep the waltzing, low-flying towplane neatly in front of me as far as possible. After I had landed - with the exam in the bag - Bill met me, grinning: *See? Worked, didn't it? Doing it when it's sunny is no challenge.* And he clapped me hard on the shoulder and

vanished into the hangar.

I almost burst with pride. A few months later, the pilot's licence was mine.

But I never forgot the Cat. I finished my degree; travelled all over the place as a pilot. With my mates, I took part in anything that had even the slightest connection with aviation. Naturally, we drove - or flew - to the major airshows as well. Back then, Ramstein was the hottest event. You could see everything there. We all wanted to go, and that's what we had planned that year.

Two days before the show, we scrapped that decision for some reason and instead went to Celle, which was closer and also hosted a popular airshow. This one even had the *Red Arrows*. And perhaps we got lucky: that was the day when the tragic *Frecce Tricolori* accident happened at Ramstein…

But of course, I knew nothing of that when we arrived at Celle. We pushed our way impatiently through the visitors in order to get as close as possible to the BF-109 - freshly restored and ready for its demonstration flight - as, up above, a Saab *Draken* proved that its afterburners made the loudest roar of any jet I'd ever encountered.

And then I saw it, hazy in the shimmering heat of the concrete apron, way at the back next to a hangar:
A Catalina.
Unbelievable. Of course, I immediately attempted feverishly to find out everything about the aircraft.

Could it fly? Where was it from? Who crewed it? I pestered the shoulder-shrugging steward by the barrier; the blonde in the info tent was really just responsible for missing children; and at the guard post, I was finally directed to the cordoned-off military-style operations tent, into which - obviously - I was not permitted.

The only thing I could finally find out was that the PBY could not participate in the flight program due to an engine failure and was not exhibited at the flightline due to the upcoming repair.

A military airfield. No chance to get on the apron, let alone near the Cat. No chance.

But I was not disappointed.

And I thought about the movie again.

A few years passed and occasionally I had the Cat in my head again and again. I flew and flew, did some ratings, accompanied a friend as a Co in a Piper Cayenne from time to time abroad and flew and flew and flew. Gliding in the Alps and in the Pyrenees, I tried aerobatics, also got the UL certificate and flew and flew. I sat in a T6 for the first time, I climbed around in a B-25 for the first time, completly dazed. And I happened to visit quite so many Air Shows, enjoying all kind of different Warbirds howling around my ears.

But I never saw a Cat again.

But from time to time I still thought about this great plane, at the latest after Steven Spielberg's *Always* with his great pictures about the old planes, which were now working for the Firefighters.

The Cat.

Events took their course. Always unexpected and with plenty of twists and turns.

One rainy, dreary autumn evening, a friend called me from the airfield. (I should mention that by then I was temping at a nearby local radio station, presenting a couple of late-night music programmes)

He told me that his flying club wanted to organise a little airshow. He asked whether, because of my radio job, I might be interested in presenting some of it. I didn't have to think about it for long before agreeing.

As the day drew near, I prepared thoroughly.

On a bright summer's day, under a blue sky, I told the crowds of visitors at the little airshow about aeroplanes and aviation. It all went surprisingly well; my friend and the audience were satisfied, and so was I.

Then, just a few days later, he called me again. He was in contact with the organiser of one of the big national airshows, whose presenter had cancelled unexpectedly. He had recommended me. Could I give the guy a call?

I took a deep breath.

I knew these kinds of events well: everything was organised as professionally as could be, and they often attracted more than 60,000 visitors.

Hell, I thought, this one's really too big for me. I can't handle it. It's totally different. Just too big.

But my friend wouldn't stop going on about it; wouldn't leave me alone. What was I supposed to do?

The very same day, shaking with nerves, I called the number my friend had given me.

The resulting conversation was actually incredibly pleasant: we quickly agreed terms and swapped contact details, and a few days later, the programme for a truly huge airshow was on my desk. Two days of presenting, accommodation, and, if they were satisfied, some money as well. Wow!

Breathless, feeling like I was going crazy, I prepared myself, and four days later, I was sitting in my clapped-out old car, heading east.

The show was an unexpected stroke of luck for me: the organiser was so happy with my presenting that he immediately booked me for five more airshows.

I couldn't get my head round it at first. Totally unbelievable. The whole apron was open to me; I was soon involved in scheduling; I got together with the pilots at the beer-call in the evenings; and sometimes I got to fly in a warbird or oldtimer - occasionally even as the copilot.

And then.

It happened at my third show, at an old Russian airfield near Berlin.

I remember it well: I had just arrived; it was a hot Friday evening in early summer and I was strolling cheerfully along the barriers, greeting a couple of people who'd already landed.

Perhaps a cold beer after the long journey, I thought.

Then I heard a noise and immediately scanned the horizon. That had to be at least two Pratt & Whitneys!

I screwed up my ears. No doubt: a really slow aircraft, still a long way away.

And then I saw it, gently backlit by the magnificent sunset; silhouetted as it flew into the traffic circuit:
the PBY. A Cat!
And I hadn't heard a thing about it! Clearly they'd forgotten to mention it in the copy of my run down.

I braced myself on a barrier as the aircraft, landing gear lowered, rumbling darkly, turned onto the base leg and, a few minutes later, engines idling and emitting that slightly offset double squeal, came down gently and serenely on its main landing gear.

It taxied along no more than fifty or sixty metres from me. I was stunned.
I stood by the barrier as though nailed there as the Cat, brakes howling, came to a stop level with me and dipped briefly onto its nose gear.
The walky-talky in the leg pocket of my flightsuit squawked. It took me a while to realise that the call was for me.
Clumsily, as though drunk, I fished the device out of my flightsuit and answered. It was the tower.
You're standing in just the right place; can you direct the Catalina to the next spot? it squawked. I thought I was about to drop the thing.
I grunted *Roger*, hurdled the barrier elegantly as never before, raised a hand briefly to the Catalina and ran like a madman to marshal it into the next parking bay. Then it braked; the engines gave a final, brief roar; the propeller spun to a halt; and the cylinders came to a noisy stop.
Some bustle in the cockpit, then the upper port cockpit window opened and the French crew clambered nimbly down to the

main landing gear via the staircase, handholds and protrusions, and from there onto the apron. A few bags were chucked neatly down from the cockpit and caught below, and at last, everyone gathered around me.

The crew greeted me cheerfully in broken but easily understandable German. Handshakes, claps on the back. Post-flight checks. Chocks on the main landing gear; back aloft to hang the oil collection containers under the engines.

I was enraptured. The first impression branded itself into my memory: the delicate crackling and rustling of the cooling engines; the long, broad curve of the rivet lines on the fuselage; the silvery colour of the metal, brittle and flaking away in places; the huge wings that bestrode the apron; the traces of exhaust fumes along the engine nacelles; the little black trickles of oil that crept across the metal behind the open cowl flaps; the big observation dome at the rear; and the diamond-patterned profile of the main landing gear's powerful tyres. I remember it all perfectly. I couldn't help but walk around the aircraft a few times, impressing every detail on my mind.

My heart beating hard: Could I possibly see the cockpit?
La porte est ouverte, I heard in reply.

I clambered up the main landing gear and the handholds on the fuselage, pushed the window open from above and climbed in, remembering to close it behind me.
It took some gymnastics to position myself above the cockpit, push open the upper window and slide down, supporting myself on the left-hand seat, until I could sit.

It's still the same: these old cockpits always have an incredible charm for me. None of the chilly sterility of gleaming multifunctional point-and-click control panels surrounded by computer keyboards; none of the impersonal digital indicators with their inane controls.

This was a neat cockpit of the old school; an uncluttered, well-ordered watchmaker's shop with everything in its place.

And yet every time I sit in these old cockpits, lost in dreams, it seems to me that the peeling labels on the black dashboard want to tell their own stories. The reflective dials of the big analogue instruments, with traces of numbers and pointers beneath them like something from another era. The metal of each black set screw has been rubbed bare in one place or another, testifying to the number of flights it's seen. Switches still seem to be switches here; the landing gear lights are resplendent behind large glass frames; the sophisticated construction of the throttle, mixture control, prop controls and trim lever above me to my right conceals a network of bare control cables behind a cluster of pulleys; behind me, an anachronistic switch box with ancient-looking voltmeters, fuses, rows of toggle switches and ventilation slits. In front of me, the huge dual control linkage: a massive U-shaped pipe with the steering wheel-like controls mounted on it, a hefty switch box for the engine and lighting settings in the middle, and below that a big magneto switch as wide as a saucer. No thin, rough plastic treads for these rudder pedals: their massive frames mean that braking or steering requires firm footwork. Far below, the green-painted, corrosion-resistant riveted ribs vanish into the darkness of the bowsprit at the front. Above it all, on the cockpit panel, hangs the obligatory magnetic compass.

Within its battered metal frame, behind a thick, deeply curved glass front, bobs a black ball with barely-visible compass markings. Even the unreadable compensation table is there - a small, faded card wedged in the bent aluminium bracket. The little GPS receiver and the new radio with the digital display on the transponder seem totally out of place; foreign bodies in this cockpit that dates back more than half a century. A stylistic incongruity.

To my right and left, beside the worn-out seat cushions, are nothing but bare ribs, bundles of cables, wire harnesses stuck to the greenish metal beneath the side windows. The switching unit, added later, seems a little pointless here. The window panels, riveted to their metal frames, have their fair share of scratches. Red kill switches and equally red lights for the fire extinguisher system blaze in the middle above the front windows. And then the smell – a unique, impossible-to-describe mixture of paint, oil, lubricant, exhaust fumes, leather and hydraulic fluid, perceptible everywhere in these big old aircraft.

I no longer know how long I spent in the aeroplane that evening. After all, I still had to inspect the observation dome, the navigator's seat and the mechanic's spot directly below the wing. I can still remember every detail.

Every single one.

The deep red sun was dying slowly behind the silhouette of the tower when I at last hauled myself out of the upper cabin window, closed it, clambered hand over hand down the handholds to the main landing gear in the twilight and finally jumped down onto the apron.

I stood there in the last light of the day, almost intoxicated by what I'd seen of the massive aircraft.

The Cat.

I was barely able to tear myself away.

Five long minutes later, I went over to the crew tent.
The same backslapping as ever; the same *get-the-man-a-beer*,
the same laughter around the tables. At last, I found the Cat's
crew in the crowd and was able to give them a standard *plane
safe and locked*.
And then the beer flowed. And the words. And the stories.

Very shyly, I told them mine - the one with the Cat. What I
had experienced, what I knew about the remaining aircraft, my
curiosity. And, to my astonishment, they listened attentively,
their eyes on me, asking questions. I was truly stunned - and
not a little bewildered - by their interest in my narrative.
Yves thought about it and, after a long pause, said, *Tu doit voler
avec nous demain. Tu sera mon Co.*

After another litre or so of beer, we decided against my
rudimentary French skills and in favour of Yves' rudimentary
English skills. He rummaged in his bag. With the words *Piilotts
scheckliist* he plonked his ring-bound checklist down onto the
spruce-wood table by my glass. Of course, I immediately began
to leaf through it, memorising it straightaway. *This is for tonight*,
he said, and I put it down again.
As expected, the evening ended a lot later than I'd planned.

I lay cheerfully in bed in the middle of the night, wading
through page after page of checklist, only learning the most

61

essential sections and skipping the emergency procedures. I began to repeat everything to myself or to look it up for the nth time…

I must have fallen asleep at some point. At any rate, the checklist was lying, still open, on the other side of my bed the next morning.

And then, barely half an hour later, I was standing in front of the aeroplane with Yves in the cool, quiet morning.
The airfield was perfectly still; the sun had only just risen. I'll never forget it: the beginning of a beautiful blue-skied day, a light mist still hovering along the edge of the woods that bordered the airfield to the north. And the quiet.
That beautiful morning.

Yves more or less led me through the outboard check by the hand and we walked slowly together around the huge craft.
Soon, we were climbing up the landing gear; I was opening up the cockpit roof again and we were lowering ourselves down inside, followed by another member of the crew, who pushed the roof closed above us and vanished towards the rear of the plane.
I sat, dazed, in the copilot's seat.
I still couldn't believe it.
I was sitting in the Cat's cockpit.
Yves undid the bulky red lock from the huge dual control and we went through the preflight checklist. I'll admit it took some time - I had to get my bearings and I was as giddy as a schoolboy.

Yves endured this with the patience of a saint, and at last we were ready to start: *fireguard posted*, circling a finger to indicate that we should start the starboard engine. Yves manipulated the starter and, once the propellers had spun nine times without catching, I switched magnets hot, and, against a backdrop of juddering noise, with wild stutters, glitches, shudders and more glitches, the first Pratt & Whitney cylinders began to work. It took a while for their speed to stabilise, for everything to be running smoothly, with a warm sound, and for us to get the manifold pressure and temperature to the right level. A few minutes later, both engines were humming loudly to themselves above us, and Yves signalled for the chocks to be removed. The throttle opened, and the mighty flying boat began to move. I could still hear the reminder not to use the brakes so much. I could hardly hide how tense I was as we taxied slowly down the endless taxiway, the Pratt & Whitneys mumbling peacefully to themselves as they idled.

We carried out the final checks and turned slowly onto the runway. Then we slowly opened the throttle above us and I gripped it firmly. The radial engines awoke with a roar and the aircraft shuddered as though impatient. Slowly, the wide propellers hauled it into the air. It accelerated sluggishly and, working at full load, the engines steadily sucked the petrol from the fuel lines. Slowly, their roaring stabilised, smooth and powerful.

Airspeed alive, said Yves, and I saw the needle of the airspeed indicator slowly rising; at a little over eighty knots, I felt Yves pulling the dual control linkage slowly yet forcefully towards him. I put my right hand on the big steering wheel, my movements almost too convulsive. The huge plane lifted off majestically; the landing gear withdrew, unbelievably slowly, with a hum of hydraulics; we gained height; I carefully reduced speed and we rose slowly above the delicate veil of fog into the quiet orange morning.

I'm certain we roared down the runway and rose into the air just as majestically as the Cat in the film, in the scene that had made such an impression on me as a boy.
I turned and looked up: the big radial engines thundered behind me, their propellers gleaming silver in the light of the rising sun. My fingers were still locked around the throttle levers above me.

It was exactly as I had always imagined. Exactly.
The kind of happiness that stuns you; that makes you forget everything else; that sweeps over you, warm; that invigorates and illuminates you.
A happiness that shows you what matters; that you'll never forget. I often think that we no longer trust ourselves to claim these sensations, to expand our experience of the world.
And yet it's so simple.

We flew in a flat circle towards the south; I could hardly free myself from this intense rapture. Below us, a forest stretched almost to the horizon. The air was still and we were climbing gently.
Yves nodded to me. I put both hands on the steering wheel, my feet found the control surfaces, and then I was flying the Cat.
I was flying the Cat!

Yves had let go of the controls and was observing me appreciatively as I ventured my first cautious movements: steering took less force than I had anticipated and the sedate craft followed my movements with wonderfully gentle languor. The engines were still droning above me; we were still climbing slightly; soon, the tips of the wings were snatching at the first light wisps of cumulus clouds around us.

Yves could only nod to me.

After all, I'd already told him everything.

I sat in the cockpit, silent with exultation. Again and again I returned my gaze to the circling propellers, the huge wings above me, the old, quivering instruments with their details of manifold pressure, height, speed and heading. Again and again I returned my gaze to the breathtaking chasm of clouds that I was piloting the vast aircraft through.

My heart was overflowing.

I was still the boy who had sat in the cinema watching the Catalina taking off on its flight to Santarém. Who was now sitting in this PBY, calm, the controls in his hands.

The propellers shimmering in the sun behind me. My body vibrating soothingly with the roar of the engines.

My heart overflowing with an indescribable happiness.

An hour later, we glided to the end of our landing, the Pratt & Whitneys once again mumbling idly.

Cat Bravo Yankee is cleared to land, wind is calm, muttered the headset.

I was steering as the huge aircraft glided comfortably in and in;

the landing nothing more than a gentle tap that hardly even seemed to ruffle my hair.

Are you okay, buddy? Yves asked.

I was clutching the throttle on the overhead panel tightly with my right hand.

All I had to do was nod. He understood.

He winked at me.

How great some gifts are...

When I started writing this story, I began to search for the Catalina from the Bud Spencer and Terence Hill film. I rewatched the DVD, which I still had lying around somewhere. I fumbled through slow-mos and stills. And I did plenty of research: it had to be somewhere, after all.

My own archive initially led me astray: the plane was listed incorrectly (somebody had probably mixed up the numbers), although in the end it did turn out to be there. There was very little information available about the filming process, but I had plenty of contacts. I wrote dozens of emails and phoned around my acquaintances.

And finally I found it: the plane still existed! Even if it was in pretty poor shape by now.

As filming mostly took place in Columbia, the film crew chartered one of the Columbian air force's PBYs. The Cat was a remnant of the US navy (construction no. 1817), sold to Columbia at the end of the 1940s. The Columbian military made use of it under the registration number FAC 619. When they decommissioned their fleet of PBYs, the 619 was acquired by an air freight company. It received the civil registration HK-2116P in 1978, flew around Columbia and South America for a few years, and was then largely disassembled by the same company to provide spare parts for a different PBY (HK-2215P/construction no. 34012, last seen in 2008 at La Vanguardia, Villavicencio (SKVV)). The HK-2116P civil registration was removed from the registers on 18 April 2000. Some friends tipped me off that there were photos of the plane from the film on the internet - the last ones, dating from 2004. The final resting place of the 619 was the edge of the Columbian military airfield in Madrid, Cundinamarca (SKMA). There the carcass stood, exposed to the elements, engines gone, airframe clearly badly weathered, tail assembly lying dismantled beside it. I heard rumours that the fuselage and the remaining components of the 619 were to be used as a restoration project for the Colombian Air Force's museum, but nobody would confirm it officially when I enquired. The only thing certain is that the 619 will never fly again.

But, after changing hands many times, the PBY I flew with is still in the air...

Illusion

Evening. The door snaps shut and I swing a leg over the centre console.

Let myself fall back into the chopper's seat. Feel for the shoulder and waist straps behind me, click them closed. Pull them tight.

Next, I grab the grey headset from its little hook above the starboard door. I leave it around my neck for now, but I do plug it into the socket.

I lean back and let my gaze wander meditatively over the welter of instruments, little switches, dials, levers, lights, controls and indicators, all imprinted with abbreviations and figures, arrayed on the consoles around me in an apparently unintelligible system. All quiet and unmoving. Dead.

The idea that I could bring them all to life with just a few trivial movements of my hand gives me a feeling of peculiar power.

I look up. On the instrument panel above me, concealed within a maze of buttons, controls and safeties, under a small red cover with the label *Main Generator*, is a small toggle switch. I snap back the red safety, lock the switch in the on position and close the flap over it again.

The effect is formidable: the aircraft seems to wake with a muted hum; individual red and white lights start to blink on, inviting me to flip more switches.

My hands begin to dance over the cockpit's keyboard: circuits close, fuel and hydraulic pumps come online - some of the red lights on the display go out again - auxiliary power units are activated, the various systems come to life one after another.

I concentrate on my flight instruments; release the lock on the artificial horizon and watch patiently as it bobs into the correct position; set the altimeter's indicator back to the zero mark; check the hydraulic and oil pressures, the voltage indicator and the fuel level. It's all ready to go.

Once again, I lose myself in the play of the countless indicators and lights. In my hand is a little pad with abridged instructions set next to long columns of numbers, diagrams and warnings: my checklist.

I murmur the long list of instructions quietly to myself like an incantation, line by line; run my fingers over the instruments and switches again; take various readings one more time.

I enter a series of numbers into my UHF transmitter control unit; finally pull the headset on; listen to the endless static of the radio. Mechanically, I press the PTT switch on the stick. The tower gives me start-up clearance. I have no need to consciously coordinate the next set of movements: left hand on the collective, opening the throttle till the engine starts idling; thumb pressing the starter button at the same moment that I trigger the cockpit clock and hear the turbine begin to howl; gaze glued to the RPM indicator where the needle is rising obediently; thumb releasing the starter.

The dozens of little needles that just a moment ago seemed frozen in place on their dials are now beginning to tremble into the green. The rotor hisses above the cockpit roof; first quietly, then ever faster. Before long, I can even hear the distinctive throbbing through my headset.

I hit the microphone button again; the air traffic controller's instructions crackle in my ear - in English, of course. I quietly acknowledge the strings of numbers, abbreviations and distorted phrases - my takeoff clearance.

Final check - everything in its place. One last look.

I open the throttle millimetre by millimetre, pulling the pitch constantly. The throbbing of the rotor becomes louder; the RPM indicator hovers by the correct mark; the needle of the torque indicator climbs slowly upwards past little white numbers.

Holding the stick lightly, I rely on my instinct; I can feel the helicopter slowly becoming as light as a balloon. It sways uncertainly on its skids like a child learning to walk. I trim it, forcing the nose down slightly; rudder against the torque; gentle movements of the stick; I pull the collective back a little further and uncouple the craft from the concrete.

And fly.

No euphoria: I have to keep concentrating. The stick in my hand drifts gently yet rapidly forward; the Bell rises higher, gathers speed; the airspeed indicator edges cautiously towards the eighty-knot mark.

I can feel my hand clenched tight - too tight - around the black plastic of the stick. Stay calm, I hear myself say through the headset. A slight curve to the right; the ADI shows I'm banking; VSI; speed; the ADF's needle swings towards the course I've set.

The controller's voice cuts, stuttering, through the static in my headset. I follow his instructions, bringing the helicopter up to the height indicated at the rate of climb he recommends, then change the frequency and switch on the radio navigation. Invisible waves and currents force themselves into the aircraft via antennae and colourful wire harnesses, moving elaborate mechanisms, indicators and columns of numbers on a little digital display. The needle of the radio compass travels slowly around the dial, steadfastly showing me the way.

Crosschecks.

Instrument values are normal, the rotor is clattering steadily, my approach chart is on my kneeboard. When I reach the appropriate distance from the beacon, I initiate the NDB Alpha approach. I use my wrist to move the stick; the helicopter tilts obediently to the side.

I would find the darkness around me oppressive if I weren't able to orient myself by the gentle red lighting of the cockpit. The shielded, dazzle-free light seems almost cosy. It's a little squally;

I attempt to correct for the slight rocking as neatly as possible, to keep the aircraft on course. I can hear myself breathing through the headset.

For almost an hour, I manipulate this construction of carefully matched aluminium parts, struts and ribs, commanding almost a thousand horsepower with simple motions of my hands. Not lifeless matter - each movement gives me the impression that the hydraulic lines, pulleys and cables, bearings and transmissions are nothing other than more detailed extensions of my arms, legs, fingers.

The air traffic controller hauls me out of my reflections; I have to react to the crumpled voice forcing its way out of the headset. I have to. Transponder codes, course directions and altimeter adjustments rapidly - too rapidly - crowd out my thoughts.

A little later, the flashing display with the message Twenty min. fuel warns me to turn back. I begin to bank; switch the navigation system to the frequency of the locator beacon. With a playful swerve to the left, I set the aircraft on its approach course. Another change of frequency initiates the upcoming landing.

The GCA controller directs me into the traffic pattern with a series of new coordinates. *Cockpit checks completed*, I confirm, and the talkdown begins straightaway.

I focus all my attention on the instruments again; the controller reels off altitude readings, courses, descent rates and distances in a relentless monotone and with merciless speed. It's all I can do to implement it all.

I confirm the landing clearance; my radar altimeter begins to move - first slowly, then ever faster - around the dial; we pass decision altitude; a yellow light flares; a warning tone in the headset; then the controller's voice cuts off abruptly, as though someone has turned off a tape.

Just a few more metres. I pull back, cutting the helicopter's speed; hover almost on the spot; push the collective slowly down; raise the nose a little. I feel the left skid touch the ground, followed immediately by the right. The airframe bucks and judders like a wild horse; I cautiously push the collective fully down until the entire weight of the helicopter is resting on its skids.

I exhale audibly and allow myself to untense and sink back into my seat for a moment.

My hands dance over the console again, switching off one system after another; the roar of the rotors changes; I reach up and pull the rotor brake down; the master switch clicks into the off position; the last humming dies away; the instruments return to rigidity.

My headset migrates to the hook above the starboard door; I snap open the harness's quick-release mechanism. With the checklist in my hand, I worm my way through the darkness of the cabin towards the rear.

The harsh neon light of the hangar dazzles me when I open the door.

Disoriented, I let my gaze wander over the black pressure lines of the hydraulic stand that forms the base of the flight simulator.

I'm still standing in its doorway.

I climb down the narrow silver ladder; the man at the control console raises a hand from inside his glass box; I nod back, tired and confused.

The illusion was perfect, I think as I exit onto the damp apron. The heavy steel door slams shut behind me.

Formation

It was a peaceful summer day in the Pyrenees, near the Spanish border. Late afternoon.

The sun hung low in the sky to the west, just above the mountains that bordered the valley. The soft late afternoon light; only a few hours left before it would sink behind the peaks. The languid stillness of the airfield succeeded the midday fervour; a tranquil updraft above the valley.

Flying together. In formation.

It wasn't planned; they just came to a decision. Nothing pre-arranged.

They simply nodded to each other, almost imperceptibly. The others didn't notice a thing.

She climbed into her glider and he watched placidly as she and her craft rose into the evening sky on the winch cable, almost soundlessly.

He closed his canopy, strapped in, checked the instruments and set off a few minutes later.

He responded to every movement of the aircraft, never losing sight of her. She was still a long way ahead of him. The variometer chimed; a shallow ascent; he turned its volume down. He could already feel it all.

He had spent many hours in the air, and yet he still drank in every moment that he spent up there. The cool softness of the clouds. The incredible deep blue above him. The battles with the weather. The dazzling sun and the reflections in the glass of the cockpit. The solitude. Beauty that took his breath away.

He was there.

And he wished himself back there after every landing.

He was always shocked by the other pilots' barroom chat and engineering obsessions. For him, heroism meant something different.

Totally different.

On your right, he said briefly, and released the microphone button again.

A fleeting crackle through the speaker as confirmation.

No more.

She knew...
Very gently, he balanced out the aircraft. She was flying just a
little way ahead of him, into the setting sun, and he glided
cautiously alongside her, metre by metre. It was perfectly simple.

He knew that she trusted in her aircraft; he trusted in her
movements.

He had a friend who he often flew with.
He could sense everything when they flew together. They
would race low over the trees at a breathtaking pace with just a
few metres separating the two of them; perfectly safe.
Aerobatics and tricky landings.
Long distances. He could anticipate how he flew. They were in
total control: crisp exchanges over the radio, precise
manoeuvres, fierce concentration, racing adrenaline, no limits,
pure feeling. And once everything was exhausted, after the
landing, they laughed. Impishly liberated, like children at the
end of a dangerous and utterly crazy adventure.

But this was something totally different.
Much calmer.

The air was still. He flew close by her.
She tinkered with the aileron, sliding a little closer. He gave her
the space to do so. He maintained height on instinct. A
fractional correction.

The wings of their aircraft almost touched. Centimetres. No
danger.

The warm evening air supported them both. Instinctive, almost imperceptible movements of the controls. He looked across at her cockpit and startled. How close…

Left, he heard her say, and the radio fell silent again.

The aircraft turned as though linked by a thread, close together; he didn't need a fixed point to orient himself by, didn't need to concentrate.

He simply flew. With her.

He wondered what they looked like from below. Whether anyone was looking at them at all.

They glided above the valley for almost two hours, the calm of their surroundings transferring itself to them.

The sun was touching the mountains by the time their aircraft broke away from each other and made their way back to the traffic circuit.

He taxied to a halt right beside her. Her cockpit hood lay in the still-warm grass beside the plane.

He opened his own, and knew that she was watching him.

Fear

Flying isn't dangerous. And yet many people are afraid of flying. Their feelings lead them to believe that it's unnatural for a thing made of tonnes of aluminium and steel to lift off from the runway.

On the other hand, they don't find it unnatural for people to speed through comparatively narrow and heavily populated streets at 180 kilometres an hour or more in a metal box on four wheels. Nobody considers that unusual any more, even though an entire village's worth of people wipes itself out that way each year.

Unspectacular.

My first flying instructor, a mischievous older man with well over 18,000 flight hours to his name and an impressively varied list of licences and ratings, used to tell me *to drive home safely after* our evening lessons.

He never said that when it came to flying.

After all, when you look at it in perspective, flying is nothing more than simple physics. Easy to explain.

It works. Time after time. Every day.

You might not think so, but aeroplanes are - statistically speaking, going by the number of passengers or kilometres flown per day - one of the safest methods of transportation. And yet air crashes do sometimes happen.

Any pilot who witnesses an aircraft meet with an accident or crash will never forget the horrific brutality of the helplessness that overwhelms them at the sight.

At any rate, I don't know of any pilot left cold by such an event.

One winter evening, I was sitting in front of the TV watching a documentary about US naval pilots in the Pacific War. As I followed these Corsairs' descent towards the aircraft carrier, I knew immediately that something was wrong. I almost stopped breathing.

The friend next to me - also a pilot - yelled frantically, *What's he doing?!*

As the aircraft swooped over the deck, I stamped on the left rudder pedal, cut the throttle and swiftly pulled back the stick. Unmoved by my attempts at correction, the F4U headed almost directly towards the camera and, just before reaching it, crashed into the deck superstructure to starboard with infernal speed.

My efforts had had no effect, although it was fairly obvious to me what the pilot could have done to avert the crash.

Every pilot experiences critical situations, hears about crashes and about people who died in their planes.

And every pilot is reckless sometimes - it's normal, and it's fun.

And every pilot who's sometimes flown recklessly is familiar with the little demon that sometimes follows you into the cockpit to whisper in your ear.
It encourages you to forget things: the preflight checks (*they don't have to be sooo careful - after all, you're in a hurry*), your weight and balance (*the runway's longer than it needs to be anyway, and the density altitude will work itself out*); your plane's emergency procedures (*it's the most reliable aircraft you know, and you only just carried out the last comprehensive check*)… and it doesn't matter if you leave your map behind this once; you know this area like the back of your hand anyway.

The demon also whispers to you when you're flying the old tub: hey, get a little closer to that tree; go inverted, no-one will see it. You can do it!
Go on, fly through that thick cumulus there; it'll be fine.
Take the turn a bit tighter and let the ol' girl shake; you're still

well within limits.

That front isn't so big; you can easily get round it...

And so on. Every pilot is familiar with it. And every pilot is familiar with the kind of situations we term *scary*.

The way your knees go slightly weak after the landing, as you realise that the demon was on the point of going too far. When you see, very clearly, that you only just pulled through – again.

We've all heard the saying: if you're not scared, you're not paying attention.

And when it comes down to it, we all know that it's true.

But we really don't get scared - except when we're alone.

And of course, we'd never mention that, just like we'd never mention the fact that sometimes, things do go wrong. After all, that might damage someone's image. Particularly ours. And that wouldn't do. Because we're pretty certain we're the coolest.

We're sure of ourselves. We take risks. We're bold. Superior. Calculating. And we're well-trained, too. We know how to fly. Who else can say as much? Well, then.

Of course, this rarely-mentioned aura is one of the reasons why we've struck the term 'death' from our vocabularies. We're as superstitious as children and we avoid the word like the plague.

If we really have to talk about it, we have cyphers, codes, just as we do for every other area of aviation.

That was well into the red, he took himself for a ride, chucked his jalopy into the woods, chopped up his crate, just wasn't cool enough, went west, he burned himself out, screwed things up, wanted to know for a fact, and, and, and...

Judgements are always close at hand for these cases: most of them were just too stupid, crapped out, wanted to play the hero, didn't have a good enough handle on things, just acted like idiots. That guy should have picked a less dangerous hobby: fishing, or something. Then it would never have happened. And we talk a lot. Too much. After all, everyone knew that so-and-so just made one lousy landing after another. And besides, he never flew enough. Not to mention that he was way too old – what do you reckon he had to pay for his medical? And anyway. It was obvious. It had to happen sometime. You could see it coming.

And everyone nods. Everyone.

It's different when it happens to someone you know well. More cutting. More solemn. More affecting. More violent.

And then, suddenly, nobody can understand it. After all, he had so many flight hours under his belt; I flew with him often enough and he never made mistakes; he was a born pilot. Everyone knows that.

Impossible to grasp.

I knew a truly excellent pilot who'd flown his entire life; an exemplary career: glider pilot, over to Sheppard with the Air Force, 104s and then Tornados with the German Navy, deputy squadron leader until his retirement, then passenger services: 727, 737, 747. Long-range with the 747s, obviously.

He went through ratings like other people collected stamps. In his spare time, he flew a Christen Eagle and took part in aerobatics competitions with considerable success.

When he retired from the passenger lines as well, he hired himself out to the maintenance yard at our airfield for fun and flew ferry flights for the businesses there - all over the place, with all kinds of planes.

I had had my licence for a few years and got to know him by chance. We got on straight away.

I was studying and low on money, so he took me with him as a copilot on his ferry flights all the time. In the most varied kinds of aircraft, back and forth across Germany and Europe. In every possible sort of weather - and the impossible ones as well.

I learned so much from him - so, so much - even though he wasn't a flying instructor.

One beautiful summer morning, he went up in a freshly overhauled P.149D and retracted the landing gear.

I can still see it: I was sitting in the long grass by the glider winch, going through a planned cross-country flight in my head.

I glanced up at him almost casually, and I was about to busy myself with something else when I saw the Pitschy dipping its right wing oddly slowly, at only 150 feet or so.

Then, just as slowly, it turned onto its back and, seconds later, still upside down, slammed into the meadow that bordered the airfield.

A brief, dull impact and a sudden silence.

No fireball or anything like that.

I sat there as though stunned. It didn't seem to have any connection whatsoever to reality. Totally surreal.

Then, suddenly, we all started running, and I don't think I've ever run so fast in my life since.

The aeroplane was upside down and we couldn't get the cockpit hood off. The pilot was hanging in his straps, oddly twisted, dead. I can still see the look of horror in those frozen eyes. Later, I heard that they thought his left aileron had jammed for some inexplicable reason.

We all went to his funeral, looking very lost. I could have screamed, I felt so awful. The others probably felt the same; afterwards, we went to the pub and stayed there till morning; hardly saying anything, just drinking. I was in shock for days; barely slept; startled awake out of dreams in which I saw, again and again, the horrified face of my dead friend in his ruptured cockpit. That's when it began.

I started to fear flying. Just a little, at first.
It began when I was sitting in my plane, preparing for take-off. It began with peculiar thoughts creeping into my consciousness, forcing me to seriously consider all the things that could go wrong. That had never happened to me before. I tried to ignore it - without success.

It got worse. I caught myself going through each check twice or three times, even though everything was fine the first time. When I started the engines and opened the throttle, my heart beat significantly faster than usual in anticipation of the old crate refusing to leave the ground for some reason, and instead tumbling into the field on the other side of the runway.
In the air, I paid more attention than ever to the sound of the engines, sensitised myself to even the slightest change in their speed. I heard irregularities where none existed.
Then I stopped trusting the instruments; kept thinking about

what would happen if my caution panel had lost power; constantly imagined unreliable varios, jittery RPM indicators or frozen artificial horizons.

Finally, I even began to fear landings - and lo and behold, my landings really did become clumsier: I came in too long and had to go around.

To put it simply, I was just flying more nervously.

It was enough to drive you crazy.

Of course, I didn't admit it to myself - after all, everyone has a bad day now and then - even though I was perfectly aware that something was wrong with me.

So I flew less and less, and although I had plenty of time for it, there was always something that was suddenly far more important than flying.

It was unheard of: I had always sacrificed almost everything to fly, and I would never have considered just lazing around at home instead before. What could I do?

I knew what was wrong. And I knew I had never been able to lie to myself.

The solution arrived of its own accord.

Some people might say it was a coincidence, but I knew it wasn't. It was one of those little nudges that we sometimes need in order to find our way back to ourselves.

Wherever they come from.

Everyone knows that.

It happened like this: we wanted to take a few days off and - like we did every autumn - fly to a little place on the Danish coast to visit friends. A nice little tradition that we were already looking forward to by the summer.

If I'd bailed on it, my mates would have noticed what was going on, and that couldn't happen.

And besides, I told myself, you need to pull yourself together.

It was a truly lovely day: high pressure; cold, but without a cloud in the sky; visibility to the Arctic and back.

The old Skylane was crammed: me in the copilot's seat to the right and the other two behind. We droned comfortably through the air; landed somewhere outside of Hamburg to refuel; drank coffee standing up under the tower; and kept going - all perfectly normal.

I pored over the maps and handled the paperwork and the radio. I was finding flying fun again, just like before. The Danish border slipped away beneath us, and twenty minutes later, we were in sight of the little airfield on the coast. Descent: we threaded ourselves into the traffic circuit, radioed the usual people, and lowered the landing gear - and suddenly, I got that weird feeling; the feeling that something wasn't right.

At first I thought it was just the stupid fear coming back, and tried to ignore it. And after all, it was only a feeling to begin with; I couldn't make much sense of it. It took me a while to realise that something really wasn't right. Beside me, my friend was steering the Skylane calmly and naturally into the long final, seemingly unconcerned: a classic powered landing with a Beech touching down way ahead of us.

I estimated the distance to the airfield; the landing clearance squawked through the headset; perhaps a mile and a half to the threshold; I ran an eye over the instruments. We were barely a thousand feet up; speed okay; oil pressure and temperature in the green; landing gear down; engine quiet, almost idling.

I listened carefully, and that very same second, as if in response, the engine began to splutter, turned irregular, caught again as we accelerated, spluttered again, didn't catch properly. I went cold all over with fear.

We had already set the flaps and we didn't have much speed to play with - not what you want at that height, and with a fully loaded aircraft.

My friend just stared out of the window in annoyance when I took the controls out of his hands and pushed them back with a vengeance. I checked the fuel gauge: we still had enough in the tank. My gaze strayed downwards, and that's when I noticed: the fuel selector switch was in the wrong position!

As soon as I saw it, I reached for it as though possessed and switched it to the correct position, then opened the throttle carefully.

For a few impossibly long seconds, the engine continued to splutter mutinously to itself.

Then the Lycoming roared obediently back to life; our speed rose; we lurched full throttle over the runway threshold, almost stalling; I decelerated; flare; and we touched down gently.

My mate was white as a sheet as we taxied to a halt. I was still gasping for breath.

My God, that was close.

Despite long discussions and recriminations, we never figured out why the tank selector switch was in the wrong position – no doubt nobody wanted to own up to it.

We toasted our survival that night, doubled ourselves up with laughter once again, behaved the same as ever.

Proper heroes.

And I kept flying quite normally, like before: the more often the better. I almost found it more fun than before.

I'm still addicted to it and enjoy each flight to the utmost.

Strange.

I still get a little scared now and again, though.

But that's no bad thing.

It keeps me alert.

That slight fear.

But of course, I never tell anyone about it.

Obviously.

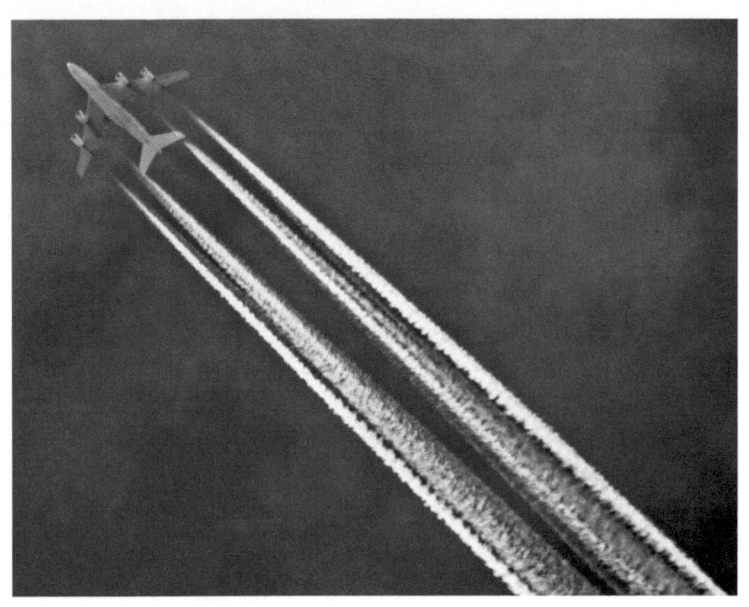

Airline

Sometimes, we let ourselves be flown. We have to. On one commercial aircraft or another, for one meeting or another. Or on holiday. It would be nice to be able to fly for ourselves every time, but unfortunately it doesn't always work that way. Unfortunately. So we fly the *line*. With a *company*.
As we say.
To explain that we're being flown, not flying.

Perhaps you're imagining that we're totally laid-back about it –

after all, it doesn't have much to do with aviation.

It's more like riding the bus. When you fly the line, you're usually above the weather and don't notice it at all. What's more, the *companies* specify the climb and descent rates and prohibit turns with more than 35 to 40 degrees of bank, *in the interests of passenger comfort* and so on.

It's not real flying. And besides, we already know how it all works.

In reality, I know very few pilots who don't ask for a window seat at check-in (and I know a lot of pilots!).

Near the wings, if possible.

Almost all of them do it, me included.

If someone we know is flying with us, we're happy to give long-winded explanations of what exactly is happening to the aircraft at that particular moment.

Or concise, cool ones. Whatever fits.

Family members acknowledge us with unfeigned boredom or endless patience when we say, for the umpteenth time, *Look outside! Isn't it amazing up here above the clouds?* or *Now he's set the flaps to 45 degrees for the final approach and we're flying at roughly 130 knots.*

As though anyone is interested.

When we travel alone, however, we just want to be left in peace to stare out of the (much too small) window. As though there were something spectacular to be discovered ten thousand feet above the thick blanket of cumulus clouds.

I still consider being able to drink good coffee while I do this to be pure luxury.

Meanwhile, other passengers squirm and groan in seats they clearly consider to be too small, and - equipped with various snacks and cold drinks - ignorantly attempt to pass the time with this or that magazine or newspaper.

Impossible.

I see things somewhat differently. Something happens every time I fly the line. Every time. And I don't just mean the spectacular experiences - though I've had plenty of those too. For example, the incredible terminal at Harare, with its swing doors leading out onto the apron. When one of the 727 freighters that landed there put on a spurt while taxiing, the doors flew open and a cloud of kerosene fumes billowed above the pitiful 1950s orange plastic seats.

Or the time that the take-off in an alarming 737 from the dawn of the airliner age caused the entire seat in front to slide onto my lap. A few minutes later, a flap above me opened and an oxygen mask descended calmly to dangle before my nose.

Or the time I had the opportunity to register as an additional crew member and to fly the Hanover-London-Paris triangle twice on the jumpseat. Take-off clearance in London: *you're number fourteen in sequence.*

Two planes ahead of us, Concorde was taxiing onto the runway.

Then, late in the evening, the overnight post to Leipzig in the same plane: an initial call in the Saxon dialect, followed by a crazy landing stunt.

My friend was absolutely determined to prove that he could make the taxiway before the middle intersection in the A320.

Once we'd touched down and the reverser had kicked in with a howl, he stepped on the brakes so hard that he pretty much pasted me to the front window.

He just about managed to hit the taxiway, but when we checked on the tyres from the ramp outside, I almost burned my fingers on the rubber.

Stories, so many stories.

Including much more tranquil ones.

Like this: One rainy, windy afternoon in late autumn, I was waiting to board at the terminal in Frankfurt. With a restorative cardboard cup of hot coffee in hand, I indulged my usual habit of pacing along the huge glass walls, watching the activity on the ramp and the taxiways.

I anticipated a short, uneventful flight back to Hanover: we'd land on time; I'd pick up my car from the car park and, after a short stretch of autobahn, return my battered, sticker-covered flight bag to its usual parking position at home. Fetch a beer from the fridge and call it a night.

That was what I was thinking about as, outside, the 737-800 followed the yellow line towards my terminal in a reassuringly slow and precise turn, braked at the appropriate marking on the wet concrete of the apron, dipped slightly onto its nose wheel and came to a halt.

Parking brake: set; both engine start levers: off; ACL and beacon: off; fuel pumps, hydraulics, flight directors, anti-ice: off; APU bleeds: on; cabin crew: informed.

I went through it all in my head. A warm, soft yellow light flared in the cockpit windows and someone jammed a folder between the control panel and the glass as the first passengers vanished into the trunk of the jet bridge, to lose themselves in the Moloch of the terminal.

Almost half an hour later, I was sitting in seat 27A with my flight bag in the locker above me. The cabin was brightly lit; a few individual passengers were looking for their places or settling more or less quietly into their seats.

The aircraft wasn't even half full. It was obvious that no-one was paying attention to the pantomime of the safety briefing, which I found fairly absurd on a domestic flight like this one anyway.

At last, the cabin lights flashed as they switched to the onboard power supply, then dimmed once the cabin crew had closed all the luggage lockers. I looked out the window at the brightly lit ramp as we pushed back and considered whether to request a coffee after take-off. The speaker above me crackled, and as the captain greeted us, I found myself laughing out loud. It was Daniel. Danny.

I had been aware that Danny flew the line. I'd known him for a while: he used to be a tug pilot when I was a glider student. He was already flying the line back then.

As a trainee pilot, I'd often flown behind with him in the tugs, and I loved it when, after releasing the tow cable, he closed the throttle with a wide, mischievous grin, pulled the nose up briefly and turned the DR 400 almost upside down - a prelude to a neat downturn which led into an equally neat nosedive, killing his height as quickly as possible. A pleasure every time. So that was who was in the 737 cockpit today. Daniel.

I didn't hesitate for long.

I reached up, found the call button for the cabin attendant, pressed it briefly.

A few moments later, a dark-haired young woman skipped up to my row. I asked her, grinning, to tell the captain that I was aboard, but only mentioned my nickname, which everyone on our airfield knew'.

This earned me a completely blank look. I repeated my request. Very slowly. I really had to get a hold of myself. Eventually, with an extremely doubtful, *Right, okay*, she disappeared towards the front.

I looked outside. We were rumbling over the ramp in the direction of one of the taxiways.

Suddenly, the stewardess was back by my row, leaning down to me as though she had something unbelievably mysterious to tell me.

The captain has invited you into the cockpit, she murmured, with an expression that suggested she'd just bitten into a lemon.

Thank you, I replied briefly, then undid my seatbelt and followed her to the front.

The other passengers eyed me with some irritation - we were already taxiing to our take-off position, after all.

At last, we reached the front and the dark-haired stewardess opened the cockpit door. I darted inside and quickly sat down on the jump seat. Danny grinned at me from up ahead. *You could have said hello a bit earlier*, he snickered, and introduced me quickly to the copilot on his right, who was concentrating on the taxiway.

Hey, I still made it in time, right? I replied, grinning. I fastened my seatbelt and looked out the window.

We were following the green lights of the taxiway. Danny braked just before we reached the threshold: we had to wait for a couple of planes to come in.

The bright dots of the approach lights flickered frenetically towards their end point, again and again. Above them hung a single piercing spotlight, which soon resolved into the illuminated outline of an A319 and landed a few hundred metres to our right. Danny opened the throttle a little, and we were on the runway.

I still find it almost indescribable, every time: the white seam of lights to each side, the equally white, sunken lights of the centre boundary coalescing into a glittering, sparkling line in the black void at the end of the runway, seemingly pointing directly into the night sky.

I was so entranced that I didn't notice we had received our takeoff clearance until I felt the aircraft jolt. The engine speed on the display in front of me rose swiftly.

The rows of lights sped past us ever faster, and soon the rumble of the landing gear cut out abruptly: we were finally in the air.

The bright airport slid past beneath us, a delicate network of lights: taxiways, runways, approach lights, end and stop lights, apron lights, parking bay lights. The undulating ribbon of headlights on the autobahn surged on endlessly as we glided towards the city centre in a gentle rightward curve. The rotating light on the tower flashed one last time before disappearing under the wings; the chequered network of lights that marked the inner city became ever smaller; and finally, even the incomparably twinkling skyline lost its shape and the steady thrust of the engines pulled us ever higher into the night sky. We'd long since retracted the flaps; Danny entered the final course and our new cruising altitude into the autopilots and grinned at me over his shoulder.

Coffee?

With milk, I replied, smiling, and he passed the order back.

He pointed out the window: we were climbing through the first patches of raincloud, ascending into the dark, hazy wall above us. In the blink of an eye, everything became as dark as night; I couldn't see a thing anymore; cautious, fitful little turbulences jolted the Boeing as we emerged from our lengthy curve and finally embarked on our course. You could only tell that the left wing was dipping gently again from the artificial horizon on the PFD. Outside, blank void.

An uncanny black wall that offered no possibility for orienting oneself.

Then we rose above this formless infinity. Wisps of cloud still clung to the winglets; the strobe lights on the tips of the wings conjured a final jerky halo from the last of the cloud; then we were through.

Far above us in the east, the bright, pale disc of the moon - not yet quite full - shed a cool light on the slate blue sheet of cloud below. As we rose, it became ever flatter, spreading itself beneath us like a bleak grey carpet, stretching out endlessly and joylessly towards the horizon. Only the moon hung immovable above it all; its bright, cold, light gleaming against our gently bobbing wings from time to time.

A few stars shimmered far above us, cool and motionless.

We had reached cruising altitude; warm cups of coffee in our hands; the lights of the instrument panel slightly dimmed; the gentle hum of the cockpit. Quiet radio chatter, hardly audible; the Warburg VOR popped up on the ND screen as the copilot stood, and, with a *your bird*, vanished into the cabin behind us. Danny glanced at the instruments, then stared out the front window into the night. Then he half turned towards me.

You know how long I've been doing this for, he said pensively, and I nodded. He looked out the front window again.

I know a lot of lads who treat it like they're driving a bus. A job. Nothing more, he continued. Pause. I could feel him searching for the words.

I think you know what I mean, he said simply. I nodded. I knew exactly what he meant.

Danny cleared his throat laboriously. *Always the same tension when I enter the cockpit. Always the same curiosity, you know?* He looked at me, briefly but directly. I nodded again, imperceptibly.

And every time this thing here pulls me up through the clouds, I get the oddest feeling. It takes hold of me. And it's big.

Pause.

I'm at home up here. I belong here. And I know it, in that moment, clearer than anything else, he said, very deliberately, and gestured briefly towards the window.

The cabin door clicked behind us and the copilot came back. I barely had time to nod imperceptibly to Danny once more.

I gazed out at the indeterminate jet black surrounding us. Almost total silence in the cockpit; my thoughts racing ahead of the Boeing with the same ease, in the same sky.

The moon was on our starboard side, untiringly bright and pale, as we flew over the Warburg VOR and Danny instructed the autopilots to begin the descent. The engines gently curbed themselves, the needles on the display swung gingerly downwards, the altitude scale changed noticeably, running steadily through the numbers. The Hanover ATIS promised the same clouds, rain and wind as in Frankfurt. Descent information came through the headset, and, following the new course, we sank towards the flat, slate blue carpet.

It wasn't long before we were flitting through the first wisps of cloud. Little bursts of turbulence gripped the aircraft again and we sank into the black void. I stared, spellbound, at the altimeter and suddenly became aware of a hazy, warm light outside, glimmering here and there among the final layer of clouds.

The aircraft freed itself from the thicket of cloud above us with a slight shake and, below, I could make out the first delicate ribbons of light that marked the streets; tiny, flickering lights moving slowly and purposefully along them.

Danny turned briefly back to me and nodded again. The copilot didn't notice. I had to smile.

The world rose up to meet us again.

I recognised the mountains, the cities, again.

Danny grunted, *I'll do a visual, ask ATC*, and, after the copilot had received clearance from the tower, the autopilot warning began to buzz and Danny hauled the Boeing left towards the airport in a broad curve. Far ahead, the approach lights strobed rhythmically at the runway threshold. The lights of the airport soon became clear.

Flap settings; the airstream tore loudly and noticeably at the wheels once the landing gear had rumbled out of the shafts; Danny swung the heavy aircraft down the glide path with slight corrections as though it were nothing; the rain raged around the front window; the blank, artificial voice of the callout droned monotonously through the altitude readings. Right after the staccato like *Retard* callout, Danny flaired the 37 carefully, the aircraft touched down slowly and gently, the engine speed shot up again briefly as the reverser kicked in, and, after a few hundred metres, we followed the green ribbon of lights down the taxiway to the terminal.

Once we'd come to a standstill and the only sound in the cockpit was the gentle clicking of the switches, and that warm, soft yellow light flared again, and the copilot shoved his documents onto the tray of the instrument panel and stood up slowly, I stayed sitting with Danny for a moment. He still had a bunch of dockets to fill out.

The cabin door clicked shut behind us again. Quietly.

You know, Danny, I said, *that was an incredibly beautiful flight. Exactly as incredible as all the others.*
Danny nodded thoughtfully.
And you're right. We're always at home up there. More than anywhere else.
He looked at me very seriously for a moment.
Safe drive home, he said quietly, winking at me again.

Thanks for the flight, I called over my shoulder as I went to squeeze through the narrow cockpit door.
Get out of here, replied Danny in an undertone.

My steps rang out on the metal floor of the proboscis-like jet bridge as I struck out pensively for the arrivals hall.
A little later, in the car park, my car door slammed shut.
Silence.

I stared quietly out the window for a moment, hands propped on the steering wheel.

What a beautiful flight, I whispered to myself, and started the car.

B - 17

One winter day, I found a letter from England on my desk. That evening, I sat down with a glass of wine and, after looking through the rest of my post, opened the envelope.

A letter. A brochure. Photos.
The letter came from a group of people who had joined together to keep a Second World War plane airworthy. It was an old American four-engine bomber, a B-17 *Flying Fortress*. The letter was very personal; none of the usual ad brochure boilerplate.
I remembered giving one of the crew members my card at an

airshow the previous year. We had been drinking coffee in the meadow in the shadow of the Fortress's huge wing, on the port side under engine number four.

The brochure featured several black-and-white photos of this plane, sometimes pictured in front of a huge hangar, sometimes on the apron and sometimes flying low over the countryside of southern England. There were a few more loose photos of the plane tucked inside in various formats.

I spread them across my desk, around the letter. They were very beautiful.

The B-17 had, it goes without saying, been restored to its original state.

The brochure also gave a brief history of the plane and its rediscovery. Built in 1945, it had fallen into disuse following the end of the war. I went to the bookshelf and took a source from my archive. This was the very same B-17 that had been used as a training craft by the air force just after the end of the war. It then served as a test platform for turboprop trials before finally being decommissioned. The dawning of the jet age had robbed it of its purpose.

The plane lay around in a depot somewhere, out in the open air, before being retooled again and sent to France as an observation aircraft. And from there, it made its way to England.

I read about the expensive, time-consuming restoration process - the pitfalls, the difficulty of obtaining replacement parts, the money troubles, the 109 fundraising campaigns, and, finally, the old plane's new maiden flight.

I was impressed by the ambition and enthusiasm of these

people I'd met at the airshow.
After all, I'm very fond of old planes, including the B-17. I'd even built a model of it as a boy – a large one, on a 1:48 scale. The Fortress hung from the ceiling of my childhood bedroom on barely visible threads, stoic and vast beside the other models, locked in a detailed aerial battle.

I'd seen the B-17 fly for the first time last year. What a strange and lovely coincidence that this letter had landed on my desk on this quiet winter evening. Even as a child, building the model, I'd hoped to one day see this plane up close, perhaps to climb inside it, or even to take a flight and imagine how things used to be, back in a time that I only knew from books of heroic stories, old photos, shaky black-and-white films. From the self-aggrandising tales told by old men at pilots' get-togethers, boasting that they'd been a part of it all.
Back then, during the war.
This was what I was thinking about as I stared pensively at the brochure on that winter evening, my glass of red wine in hand.

What was it like, what was it really like, how serious had it felt? What was it like?

What would it have been like for me back then, in the spring of 1942?
What if I'd grown up in the country somewhere in the southern US? Perhaps my patriotism and my passionate love of flying would have driven me to volunteer for the Army Air Force as soon as I'd left school. Perhaps I would have passed the medical; perhaps I would have slogged my way through the

more or less worthless basic training in one of the many camps. Perhaps.

Perhaps, when I finally made it to basic pilot training, I would have toiled through the Texas skies above Brooks Field in a PT-17 with a know-it-all army flight instructor breathing down my neck. Tests, studying, more tests. Flying. And studying. And tests.

My first solo flight - I sung, yelled, laughed. Totally crazy. Just like everyone else.

And then the wings. My wings!

Full of pride, I took my licence home with me on my few days' leave. To the South.

To my parents. I was a pilot!

I still remember the stares when, clad in my uniform, I entered my little backwater hometown's bar with my father. The old farmers were perched along the counter like chickens at roost. All the others were at war.

The brightly polished wings gleamed above the flap of my left breast pocket. *Boys*, said my father, *my son's a pilot now*, and he nodded deliberately. A brief murmur of approval; someone pressed a double whiskey into my hand; then they all raised their glasses briefly.

I was a pilot.

Shortly after that, I received my assignment. Flying bombers was much harder and more challenging than flying fighters, or so they told us. And I seized the opportunity. *Transition training*.

After nine months of training, I was introduced to the B-17.

The B-17! The Fortress. The most modern plane! Flying, training, studying, studying and flying. Fifteen weeks of training; almost 200 flight hours.

Onwards to combat training, or Operational Unit Combat Training, as they called it. To Pyote, Texas.

Tactical flight.Instrument flight. Hour upon hour. Day and night.

The promotions. And finally: Captain. Of the B-17.

I was very proud, very hungry for war. Very proud. And, of course, like all the others at the base, I was wild to know when we were finally leaving.

The first deployment.

I leaned back and looked out the window. It was the middle of the night, and it had begun to snow. Next to the wine glass lay the brochure. I stared at its pictures. Around me, all was still. And the black-and-white photos in front of me slowly filled with life, ever more life.

Perhaps (finally, finally, finally) I would have been sent to England with the Eighth Air Force. We would have flown, unlike the squads who had to endure an interminable, storm-tossed Atlantic crossing on a stuffy, overcrowded troop carrier. Perhaps we would have been assigned a brand new B-17F at Scott Field, Illinois. Straight from the factory. Only 12 flight hours in the log. Everything new, gleaming, unused. My Fort.

And even more training; preparations for the long ferry flight to Scotland. My crew came together. A good team. Good kids. From every corner of the States.

Instrument flights by day and night; calibrating *our* B-17's systems; the first, endless flights over water.

Then preparing ourselves for the leap across the Pond, as we called it. First, to Gander in Newfoundland, Canada. There, we carried out the final checks; a tense burst of activity before crossing more than two thousand miles of desolate ocean to Prestwick, Scotland. The first stop. Uneasy sleep. Will it all go to plan; is there something I've forgotten? My responsibility to my crew. Just don't screw it up.

Could I do it? Could I really do it?
But everything went almost ridiculously well: we set off in ideal weather conditions, far above the clouds, only catching a glimpse of the bleak waves far below every once in a while. And, many hours later, we taxied to a relieved halt on Scottish soil.
And then off to the war.
To our new home base.
A flight to the south of England in more or less calm weather, above this beautiful, broad, green, flat land with its scattered villages connected by narrow roads. Countless fields, bordered by hedges, formed a huge jigsaw puzzle below us, reaching to the horizon. Now and again came a shower of rain, drawing a grey curtain between us and the view below.
And then, in amongst it all, one of those airfields. Our airfield. Among the many others that we had passed over during the course of almost two hours, looking down, astonished, at the incredible mass of planes. Our airfield. Located near a low, hunched, grey English village that might be called Chelveston,

or Knettishall, or Thorpe Abbotts, or Franglingham.

The sky is turning grey.
Wooden signs with tactical symbols; white-painted stones
marking off branching paths that lead to whole rows of Nissen
huts, tents and flat, hastily assembled barracks. The wind shreds
the dirty smoke as it pours from their narrow chimneys. A vast
base bedded in the breadth of southern England.
One of the many hundreds of airfields conjured from nowhere
during the war, springing up like mushrooms. All formed on
the same pattern: beyond the guardhouse lie the HQ, the
barracks, the canteens, the briefing huts. Further out, the wide
runways, intersecting at an angle of almost 60 degrees,
connected at the ends by the perimeter track which winds
around the entire airfield like a ring road. The perimeter track
links the loop hardstandings for the bombers, which are
scattered around the site. To the south, on a small apron, stands
a simple, boxy one-storey brick tower with an external staircase:
the gallery.
The connecting roads to the enormous T-2 hangars; the repair
shops. Behind them, the guardhouse and, a little way outside
the airfield, the lodgings and mess rooms.
Hidden somewhere in the woods lie the bomb and amunitions
dumps.
A new world. Different from what I 'd been expecting: raw,
cold, grey, wet and forbidding.
I just stand there for a while, bewildered and curious.
Everyone traipses around on bikes between the hurtling Willys,
seemingly without any particular destination in mind, bags or
basic toolboxes hanging from their handlebars. Everyone here

seems to own a bike.

Finally, we come to a halt outside our quarters.

Us. The rookies.

A sergeant assigns us our lodgings: one large room for the rank and file, and one each for us officers in the Nissen huts. A cold, narrow, tiny room off an even narrower corridor, with a window, bed, table, chair and cupboard. No shower, no toilet. We've arrived.

At war.

Soon it's off to the mess for a welcome from the commander. A few brief, emphatic words. The timetable for the coming days; orders.

We're still the rookies. The beginners. Hardly worth their attention.

We're paying attention to them, though: their taciturnity, their tired gazes, their disquiet. Their trophies; the unapproachability that we still naively interpret as coolness.

And where the hell did they get those Irvin jackets??

The second day, and the first flight. Flying, flying, flying. Training. And more training. Formations and tactical formations, and formations and more formations. Tight formations. Very tight. Woe betide anyone who breaks rank. Lines of attack, navigation flights, landing procedures. The bad weather in Europe gives us trouble: cold and windy, with a low cloud base. Rain. So much rain. Truculent fog that refuses to lift even when the sun twinkles through the few narrow holes it's carelessly left. Some days, we can't even fly and instead have to sit through lessons until the afternoon. We spend these evenings bored, freezing and soaked to the skin, sitting around smoky, potbellied stoves in our cold Nissen huts. Counting the hours. Reading. Writing. Or drinking beer in the mess.

The first advice from the old hands: do this, forget that. You can ignore all of that training bullshit. Here, you're flying with the rest of us. In a cloud of B-17s. In the most bad-tempered weather in the world. Watch out for your own arse. Always stay alert. Never rely on anything; things always go differently to how you expect. And once the mission's done, you're on your own. Just get home safely.

That's all.

We marvelled at them.

I still remember that.

I remember the rest of it as well.

The afternoon of a beautiful early summer day. That day's training flight hadn't been bad at all, and I was sitting by the plane with my crew after a short debriefing. The sun already felt pretty warm, so we were sitting in the half-grown grass looking over at the runway.

As I said, it was late afternoon. The time before planes start coming in to land. They were due to arrive back from their missions on the continent soon. Like every other day. Everyone spends this period tense, walking nervously and affectedly around, watching the horizon, listening for the drone of the engines. Everyone.

And then they were there.

Just a few barely visible, barely audible dots on the horizon at first.

Coming home.

Everyone dropped what they were doing and grabbed their bikes or ran for the airfield. Like every other day.

To count the planes. To see whether they'd all made it back.

A peaceful tableau: soft light over the many fields and hedges; the colourful sky heralding the evening.

And the tiny black dots on the horizon against the low, warm afternoon sun - barely visible. Slowly, they drew closer. Soon, we heard the familiar, all-encompassing soundscape of the engines. They merged into the traffic circuit, leaving wide gaps between them.

Red Cross vehicles on the grass by the runway, engines running as the first planes landed.

Bumpy, but safe.

Then the waving arms, the cries...

Coming from the tail of a solitary Fortress with a thick, oily trail of smoke coming from engine number four, and engine number two dead. As the plane thundered across the threshold, I saw the tattered rudder, the gleam of torn metal on the port side where the radio operator would sit. I saw how an armada of wailing Red Cross vehicles shot across the runway in the wake of the plane. The Fortress taxied on into the grass beside the runway and came to a halt in total silence, engines smouldering. I heard the broken, heart-rending cries over by the Red Cross vans, which had stopped far behind the smoking wreck, looking small as toys beside it.

The humid air wrenched the sound towards us across the quiet airfield.

What happened to them? I wondered.

But I quickly forgot the profound shudder of horror that ran
through me in that moment.

Some planes landed with tattered rudders or elevators; others
had had their entire forward gunner sections ripped away by
frontal attacks and the area beneath the cockpit looked like a
slaughterhouse.
Yet others crash-landed because their landing gear was
destroyed or only descended on one side.
Or they didn't come back at all.
It all made a deep impression on me. All of it.

It was beyond understanding, imagination, description.
I heard later that one of the incoming Fortresses had no
hydraulics and only partial electrics. It couldn't get its landing
gear down either; I saw it belly-land.
All the damage - plus an almost direct flak hit - had jammed
the ball turret, and the gunner could no longer move it enough
to clamber into the belly of the aircraft. He was stuck, badly
injured and without his parachute, in the cramped, immovable
pod beneath the fuselage. And to top it off, the landing gear
couldn't be deployed manually anymore either. The pilot cut two
engines to save fuel and gain time, and circled the airfield until
the tanks were dry, but nobody could free the trapped gunner.
Nothing could be done.
Nothing.
The pilot had to land. He had to. He attempted to land the
plane on the grass beside the runway, but it didn't make any
difference. As soon as the plane hit the ground, the gunner and
his turret were crushed.
He had just turned 19 and had completed 15 missions.

We later learned that he had got to know a girl from the neighbouring village and had introduced himself to her parents the previous week.

The pilot who made the emergency landing wasn't in a fit state to fly for the next two weeks.

He just drank and drank. Then he was discharged.

How could anyone forget that? Impossible.

But we were used to it. Or so we thought. Used to the wrecks along the runway, which had vanished as though by magic the next day.

But the black, burnt patches in the grass beside the concrete remained visible from the traffic circuit day after day. We thought we would get used to it. No-one gets used to all of that. No-one.

And then our first real missions began. Milk runs, they called them. Quick hops across the Channel to France; recces or weather observations. Over and over. Those trips were pretty unspectacular – leaving aside the anti-aircraft fire along the Normandy coast. But we knew where the batteries were and simply climbed too high for them to reach us.

The fighter planes we feared never materialised. But our initial fears were hardly part of the routine.

And I loved the plane. Every switch, every instrument, every vibration. The soothing, sonorous roar of the engines. I noticed every single change in engine speed. The control forces pressing at the yoke. Suddenly familiar, all of it, a part of me.

Like a new sense.

The first bombardments. Over France. The targets were a couple of crossroads, a few railway junctions.

As always, the plane rose when the bombs tumbled from their shafts as though relieved of a burden, and we had to fight to hold it down and stay in formation. Far below, made abstract by distance, lay the swathe we had cut across the land, visible from afar thanks to the vast trails of smoke and the fires that followed the explosions. We left death, destruction and suffering in our wake. But we didn't think about that. Or only rarely.

Perhaps from time to time.

When we turned back towards England, all we felt was relief.

On the way home, you're on your own. On the way home.

You've got it good, said the old-timers. You don't have to go to Germany. Just milk runs.

One day, two German Messerschmitts roared right through our formation - without shooting at us, oddly enough.

That was off Le Havre, almost before we'd left the Channel coast behind us.

We were totally stunned, shrieking down our headsets in confused fury. By the time we'd got a hold of ourselves again, they were gone. The whole thing had taken twenty, perhaps thirty seconds. No shots. There and gone again.

We'd seen them. Clearly.

We landed feeling on top of the world - heroes. After all, we'd seen them. The Messerschmitts that everyone talked about. That everyone feared.

The intelligence officer who we reported this to at the debriefing simply shrugged. And he wasn't the only one. Late that afternoon, we went out as usual to count the returning planes. Making their way home.

Fifty-four had taken off just before us.

Thirty-eight came back. No more.

Thirty-eight.

No reports of landings from nearby airfields.

Thirty-eight.

Sixteen planes didn't make it back that day.

Sixteen crews.

One hundred and sixty men.

One hundred and sixty.

And then we were off to Germany. The very next day.

They told us at the morning briefing. Just after breakfast.

I'd spent the previous evening in the officers' mess with the others, lingering in a tatty armchair or at the battered bar, trying to numb my loneliness and my fear of this war with high-proof booze and heroic speeches.

The walls shining with oil paint and hung with trophies, sketches of blonde girls with disproportionately voluptuous bosoms, woodcut caricatures of heroic deeds.

As we did after every mission, we raised a glass to those whose planes now lay, smashed and smouldering, somewhere on the continent. Friends who had toasted the very same speeches with us the previous evening, downed the same drinks – and who were now likely either imprisoned or dead.

We tottered back to our quarters alone and halfway drunk and attempted to snatch a few hours' sleep, hoping to escape the constant confused, agitated dreams. We woke at four after one of those short, damp late summer nights you got in England, overtired and worn out by the experiences of the previous day. After some scanty grooming, we stumbled the few hundred meters in the dark from our poorly insulated semicircular Nissen huts to the mess for breakfast. Still half asleep, we washed down our bacon and eggs with cups of foul coffee, and, barely an hour later, joined the other crews in the poorly-lit briefing room.

Outside, it was still dark. A typical morning in southern England, in other words: clammy and clinging, a blanket of thick fog draped across the airfield and the broad surrounding fields, our Fortresses wraithlike in the first soft light over the hardstandings.

The base has been awake for hours: Jeeps and trucks tearing noisily through the mud; the dangling lamps in the briefing room spreading their sombre light; the men lolling wearily in their chairs; muted chatter that cuts off only when the door slams open violently.

Everyone hauls themselves upright; the CO bustles down the narrow aisle with the meteorologist and the operations officer, and clambers onto the makeshift stage. He gestures curtly to indicate that we can sit down again.

Like at the cinema, a curtain is drawn aside and a large map appears, covered in colourful lines and marks. As ever, the commander's short speech is embellished with the kind of encouraging exhortations we're now deaf to.

The operations officer points out our flight path; explains when we'll rendezvous with our escort fighters and the possible routes and backup airfields; gives us frequencies, schedules, instructions for taxiing and takeoff.

We're going to Germany. Our first mission there. It's almost a shock.

At last. Today.

Tension creeps in, rapidly banishing the exhaustion, though somehow we can still feel it lurking.

Now it's the meteorologist's turn: stable, high-pressure conditions; nothing to worry about.

End of briefing. The navigators and bombardiers remain seated for the nav briefing.

The rest of us exit into the dawn. The first light of day is slowly slinking above the damp horizon. The backlit fog hangs flat and feather-light above the fields. Like a painting.

I swallow. My body suddenly feels very heavy.

We're going to make it. Of course we're going to make it. It's our first mission.

We were still telling ourselves the same thing on our tenth. And our fifteenth. It's what we all thought. We'll make it. They won't get us. We're the best crew. For sure. Superstition. Rubbing the colourful, confident murals painted on our fuselage.

A minor, reassuring self-deception. Over and over. Because really we knew that wasn't how it worked.

By now, the bombs have been placed on board our aircraft, the weapons loaded, the fuel tanks filled, but it's still not yet time to take off. More damned waiting. Nervous back-and-forth bustle;

restless, pointless rummaging; one cigarette after another. The corrosive mixture of tension and exhaustion makes us edgy and aggressive. All thinking the same thing: Will we be back here in ten hours? Who's in for it today? What will happen? What?

Together with my crew, I pedal my old bike through the swathes of cold, heavy fog to the barracks to pick up our equipment: flying jackets, guns, flightsuits, parachutes, life vests. We throw our things into a Jeep and speed along the taxi track until we reach our Fortress. A flying monster, armed to the teeth: a thirty-metre wingspan, almost 5000 horsepower in the engines, thirteen .50 calibre Brownings. And two tonnes of bombs in its belly.

I head for my plane. Patches of greenish-brown paint peel from its glossy metal skin. Behind the engines, the wings are black with soot from the exhaust plumes. The turrets are still misty from the damp morning air.
The wheels of the landing gear still locked into the brake blocks. Outboard check. Little drops of damp fog trickle from the matt black propeller blades.
We run critical, trained eyes over air ducts, profile surfaces, control surfaces, locking mechanisms, brakes, flaps...
I open the portside hatch directly below the cockpit, toss my equipment inside and then jackknife up behind it with an elegant, practised movement. I crawl up through the narrow corridor into the cockpit and sit down heavily in the pilot's seat. The others, too, are thrusting themselves into these metal tubes, closing all the doors and getting into position for the startup checks: copilot, gunner, radio man, navigator - a total of at least

ten men.

I stare through the steamed-up cockpit window at the hazy airfield beyond for a while, tired, heedless of my surroundings, until my copilot starts fumbling loudly - much too loudly - with his seatbelt beside me.

I complete the radio check and transmit today's code to the tower. *Tower, three-six-seven for radio check: Charlie, Delta, November, Victor, Tango, Oscar, over.* The controller confirms it. I order the various men in our plane to confirm their status, then run through the startup checklist. *Prop area clear, parking brake set, generator off, fuel pump on, hydraulic system on, primer as required, throttles idle, cowl flaps open.*

And then we wait.
And wait. And wait.
Finally, the startup clearance flare goes up, and we fire up the engines, one after another. *Chocks away, taxi checks.*
Or the white flare: mission aborted. Bad weather at the target.
Gruelling waiting.
And waiting. And waiting. And waiting.
And then perhaps the flare signalling that we should taxi; the wan yellowy-orange morning sun to the east through the wispy banks of fog; *brakes released*, throttle open; the plane juddering as it taxis; the marshal waving me left onto the taxi track; slotting ourselves into an armada of taxiing planes; working the screeching brakes as the jolting chases away the exhaustion.

The plane shudders with the vibration of the engines.
We taxi onto the runway; startup checks; tailwheel locked.

A green flare back by the hangars. Pedal to the metal and we're off: our old banger, fully laden, motor screaming, hobbles over the broad concrete strip, much too slow and sluggish; finally picks up some speed; seems to cling tenaciously to the ground. Exactly thirty seconds behind the previous plane.

Just as I do every time, I wait, unbearably tense, for the first shift of the control surfaces. The tailwheel lifts off in slow motion.

And still the thing refuses to fly; the engines roar at full speed; in the midst of the nerve-shredding struggle, my calculations are clear and incisive. All the instruments are jittering frantically up and down their scales, the airspeed indicator seems to have long minutes to go before it edges into the green, and the runway is getting shorter by the second. And yet, long before we reach the end of the colossal concrete strip, the tailwheel lifts fully and I draw the yoke carefully toward me, millimetre by millimetre. The plane peels sluggishly from the ground. Pressing it gently down... more speed, more speed...

The landing gear skims fences and hedges. A barely perceptible ascent. The wheels rumble back into the engine nacelles. Restless glances through the windows. The air filled with hundreds of planes - not just from our own airfield. Hundreds of planes and no radio traffic, no flight controller. Just furious concentration.

The bomber ascends cautiously into the calm morning sky above this gentle southern English landscape. We climb together through the clouds at 300 feet per minute, following our leader. Routine checks, oxygen masks on, radio silence.

The planes gather together slowly, close ranks. Weapons checks once we reach the North Sea. The Brownings rattle away, tearing at our nerves.

Always the same, but worse now than ever.

Then they fall silent, replaced by a heavy quiet.

Swing music buzzes through the headsets; a nice warm lazy Benny Goodman ballad from some station the radio operator has picked up.

Up above the clouds, our formation drifts serene and sparkling through the dazzling sunlight as though on some wonderful excursion. The steady, comforting hum of the engines is audible again.

As though in some bright, peaceful painting, we sketch endless cascades of contrails through the cool blue of the sky.

It's almost like we're doing this for pleasure, I think.

How beautiful it is up here.

How peaceful.

How dreamlike.

The music from the headsets soon blurs into faint crackling, and then all that's left is the steady, sonorous roar of the engines all around us. Radiant deep blue sky above. The contrails still swirling playfully behind. A blanket of cloud far below. Dazzling sun, and occasionally the flash of a reflection from the other planes around us.

A signal from the navigator crackles in the headset. We've reached the designated rendezvous point, but no matter where we look, the fighters are nowhere to be seen. Fear creeps back into the cockpit. I can sense it in our rattling gasps behind the oxygen masks, in our gazes, our nervous fidgeting, our feigned self-command.

Still, the exhaust plumes of our planes condense instantly against the crystal blue sky, and we weave a wild web through the air.

Visible for miles.

And not just for our allies.

The AA guns won't go easy on us, either. We pull out our flak jackets; put on the bulky steel helmets.

Ahead of us lies the Dutch coast; the Frisian islands scattered before it like pebbles cast into the sea. And our fighters are finally here; a Mustang screaming through our midst on a knife-edge trajectory, close enough to touch. Further off, I see eight fighters circling above the bombers in formation.

Things are getting serious. They'll be waiting for us.

From far ahead come the first flak shots: tiny, dirty brown clouds that appear suddenly and hang harmlessly in the air for a while before being blown away by the wind. They all float at roughly the same level, multiplying rapidly. We climb slightly. My hands claw at the yoke. We rise slowly – too slowly – above the band of flak shots, squint at the horizon. Below us, the coast. We change course. Not far now.

Is that how it would have been? I glance outside. The snow's still falling, soft and quiet.

I put down the brochure, feeling as though I'm waking from a long dream. Wine glass in hand, I go to the large window and gaze out into the winter dark.

I suddenly remember a couple of flights I took in a TB-25D. I was sitting in the copilot's seat, battered, shuddering yoke in my right hand, throttle in my left, both feet jammed against the control surfaces. Constantly glancing out at the engines, which roared just a few feet away, and back at the spread of dials in front of me. Crosschecks.

Yes. It probably was like that, back then.

Control forces demanding your strength and attention every second. Powerful aeronautical intuition. The ability to predict what was about to happen.

Instincts keyed in to the sound of the engines.

This is not easy.

A little later, I flew in the rear gunner position of the same plane. I sat on a kind of oversized bike saddle with no seatbelt; crammed between the low turret above me, the gunsight and the huge double machine gun with its ammo feed to the left and right, and the mobile trigger between my legs. I had an incredible view between the two tail units and took hundreds of photos.

I sat there for a little over an hour. It was very uncomfortable and I was a long way from the others; separated from them by a narrow crawlway over the bomb bay: slim rungs above bare, vibrating metal. The dark green riveted panels surrounding me; the ribs, cable harnesses and control cables above, shaking from the roar of the engines.

I sat back there. It was a beautiful warm summer's day, shortly before sunset, and I marvelled at the sky. We circled Berlin; the sun flashing off its lakes and off the Havel's tributaries every once in a while. As I said, we flew for just over an hour.

It was a peaceful flight in an old bomber on a quiet evening. Nothing more.

Nodding to myself, I went back to my desk, poured some more wine and went back to looking at the photos.

Perhaps we would have headed for our target. How would it have gone?

Once we hit Holland, we would have been within range of the fighters, who were surely already lying in wait for us. For the stoic convoy flying in to bombard their cities, their fatherland. What would it have been like back then, in the spring of 1942? What if one of those fighter pilots had grown up in the country somewhere in northern Germany? Perhaps his patriotism and his passionate love of flying would have driven him to volunteer for the Luftwaffe as soon as he'd left school. The Battle of Britain may have ended in defeat for Germany, but it still created heroes.

After the more or less worthless basic training, he would have made it to an A/B school, where he would have learned to fly light aircraft such as the Klemm 35, the Focke-Wulf 44 and the Bücker 131. And because so many pilots were needed, this reduced and rudimentary course of study would have been enough for him to obtain the coveted Luftwaffe pilot's licence. Next would come fighter pilot training. In the 109. Or the 190. The countless crashes at takeoff and landing. The older, more experienced pilots in disbelief at the inadequacy of today's training programmes. The senseless losses of the first few missions.

They are below us, waiting to make the torturous ascent, to throw themselves on us in a pack.

We soar over the country, visible to anyone who cares to look. A calm tableau, for the moment. But our own calm has long since vanished. My demands to know our position and that of the initial point are becoming more and more impatient. Another endless twenty-five minutes.

And yet we make it there without incident. The wide-open sky is a radiant blue under the fierce sun as I hand control to the bombardier. Behind me, the hatches of the bomb bays open and the air rages loud and wild through the cabin. The bombardier pushes aside the safety flap of the little switch to his left, and with a flick of his finger, more than two tonnes of explosives hurtle down towards this burning city on the eastern edge of the Ruhr. Inescapable.

We can't comprehend such destruction; can't imagine suffering on such a scale.

Nor can I think about it right now. All I can focus on is the liberating upward jolt; the sudden silence as the hatches close, cutting off the rush of air from the bomb bays. The whole formation pivots into a broad rightwards curve.

I'm on my own now. Heading home. Almost relieved. Grateful for every mile we put between us and our target. Every shuddering minute of the journey back.

We're not there yet. Still alert. Yet nothing happens. It's almost too easy, our steady westward drone. Soon, we can make out the Dutch coast up ahead, swathed in a light mist.

Suddenly, the fighters scream into our midst. Out of nowhere. A full-frontal assault, at impossible speed. I need to stay the course, just stay the course. A diabolical racket of high, startled, fearful cries bursts through the intercom. Machine gun fire everywhere, the roar of the engines, almost shattering my concentration.

And then it's over. Cut off abruptly. Just the deep boom of the engines. The all-clear from each station: we're fine, they didn't get us. And yet I can't catch my breath. My fingers fumble helplessly at the mic button. Crosschecks. Everything functions flawlessly. It's all over.

Only now do I look outside. A thin, light grey ribbon of smoke trails the plane to the left of us. Engine number three. The plane descends a little, slowly falling behind.

But all its engines are still working.

It doesn't look too bad.

Suddenly, a gigantic explosion shatters the slackening tension. Our plane shudders as a firestorm flares abruptly around it. The left wing of my B-17 is wrenched upwards by the force of the explosion. On pure instinct, I brace the battered aileron against it. It takes all my strength to stay in formation. Shrapnel rains down loud and knife-sharp against our fuselage.

Once I'm over the initial shock, I glance quickly to port again. The other plane has vanished. A swiftly dissipating cloud of smoke; wreckage flashing in the sun as it tumbles away. Far below, an entire wing, engines still running, swirls sluggishly toward the ground like an autumn leaf.

I gasp for breath. My entire body is shaking.

We override the radio silence. Three other planes were hit. Two are still in the air; the third is on its way down with wing tanks ablaze. We only saw two people make it out before it dismantled.

And then we hit the Channel.

The white cliffs of Dover are a thin, impossibly bright line up ahead of us in the afternoon sun, and soon England lies beneath us once again.

Down below, they'll be racing to the airfield as always, staring into the sky to the south; the ambulances waiting, engines running, at the side of the runway.

Someone will be searching for the dots on the afternoon horizon, counting aloud like a children's game.

After a day like this, the landing really does feel like child's play.

Almost laughably routine. Always. Into the pattern, final checks, wheels out, flaps, over the threshold, pulling the throttle carefully back, and letting the plane taxi.

Into the parking position, engines off. The quiet clatter of metal as we finish up in the cockpit.

I drop through the door, astonished at how warm it is here in the mild English afternoon sun.

I let myself collapse into the grass, utterly exhausted.

We made it. We made it back.

And the German fighter pilots? Are they, too, collapsing into the grass of their airfield next to their planes following the landing? In the peaceful north German afternoon sun? They survived it, too. They made it back - or most of them did.

Will they be able to celebrate their victories? Will the crew chief paint another mark on the empennage for the plane that exploded on my port side?

And what will the wife think, standing in her pretty garden and carefully cutting flowers for a bouquet, when she sees the Luftwaffe Kuebelwagen approaching through the mild evening air? How will she feel, when the smartly dressed orderly descends from the vehicle, walking measured and much too slowly towards the gate? To tell her that her husband didn't make it back from his mission today. He died heroically. In the defence of the fatherland.

How to describe her disbelief at the sudden loss of her beloved husband? How?

How to endure such a thing? How?

No-one dies heroically. Not even her husband. He died screaming in indescribable fear, trapped in the cockpit of his shattered 109. Plummeting uncontrollably, upside down, towards the peaceful green forest below.

I walk slowly around my Fortress; fingers trembling against the metal of the huge aircraft.

I stare into the warm, bright late afternoon sun, deathly tired.

Outside the window, the snow is still falling, gently covering the fields in innocent white. All is still. I stand there, staring out, my glass in my hand. There's a lump in my throat that even the wine can't dissolve.

It's partly because I know that I can't really understand the things I'm imagining. That I can't truly have any idea of them when I live such a sheltered life.

Feeling dazed, I turn back to the desk; sit down before the photos, the books, the pictures of my children.

Another glass of wine? Why not?

And then?

Perhaps I would have survived the next mission too. Perhaps I would have seen more horrors than I could bear; more unimaginable things that nonetheless burnt themselves irrevocably into my soul.

And then?

And then my part in it all would have come to an end. At last. How we celebrated! Saved! Or were we?

Perhaps I'd simply had more luck than the others.

More luck. More luck?

How many didn't make it back?

Torn to pieces in the air or pitched into the ground at furious speed, dying harrowing deaths that we knew nothing of. Escaping their plummeting craft, relieved and hopeful, only for their parachutes to stay closed or burn up brightly above them in the blink of an eye, leaving them crashing helplessly to earth. Or gliding gently down through a peaceful sky that seemed wholly disconnected from the battle above them, making a successful landing only for their relief to turn to astonishment and horror as they were lynched by those who found them. Patiently enduring soul-destroying confinement and the wretchedness of the war in the enemy's prison camps. Lucky? Was I just lucky?

And then?

Nobody thought about them. About what happened to them all. We lived at the base. The priorities were family, home, country. The end of the war had us drunk with happiness. The dizzying relief, like a door into paradise had cracked open. Finally over, over, all over. Finally. We had no idea what came next. What it all meant.

Back home? Where?

With everything that had happened to me, I'd almost forgotten the place I'd called home.

Somewhere in the southern US.

And then I found myself in a B-17 once again. Flying back across the Atlantic with my luggage, as a passenger. A free flight back courtesy of Army Air Forces Air Transport Command, with the bomb bay full of bags. A ferry flight. Once again, the powerful, soothing roar of the engines seeped through me. Exhausted, I leaned my head against the vibrating metal and fell asleep.

We landed on one of those massive bases down south; I clambered through the rear door of the Fortress with my things, into the heat and humidity of the afternoon. The B-17 stood on the ramp, looking dreadfully lost. Nobody was there to pick me up. Home? Was I home now?

A few days and a long train ride in dress uniform later, I reached my parents' house.

My mother breaking down, my father very quiet.

The war was over. A few parades. Medals. And then? A few weeks later, I was discharged from the Air Force.

There were hardly any jobs to be found; everyone was returning from the war. Everyone wanted work. Anything they could get. Pilots were no longer anything special; there were plenty of them around. But no jobs.

I was disillusioned by this post-war life. At home. Everything seemingly peaceful. Seemingly well-ordered. Seemingly happy. Suddenly, the things we'd experienced, the horrors that had burnt themselves into our souls, were no longer of interest to anyone. Nobody wanted to hear it. We were in peacetime now. I spent a few weeks in this restless, agitated state that no-one could truly understand.

Inescapable nightmares.One day, I set off again. Perhaps to Walnut Ridge in northern Arkansas. Or Kingman in Arizona. And there I found them. Hundreds. Thousands. Endless rows of B-17s. Weatherbeaten; some with engines, some without. Long rows out in the open air.

Dismantled engines, propellers, guns, empennages from planes of all kinds. Sorted neatly, ready to be crushed for scrap.

I wandered for hours between the B-17s. Spread my hands against one of them, fingers trembling as I touched the metal of the huge aircraft.

Tears in my eyes.

Much later, I managed to create a good middle-class life for myself.

I really succeeded at it: a wife, children, a little house, a nice car, a secure job in some small southern town. But my head was still full of the war. Both the nerve-shredding howl of the guns and the soothing roar of the engines. The strained, wearying waiting and the tense approach to the target. Every time.

And then came the air show. At some Air Force base nearby. I was invited. Because I was a veteran, as they called us now. Someone who had survived it all. A hero.

It shook me to the core to stand before a Fortress once again. A G-type. Polished to a high sheen.

Someone came to my assistance, asked me to step inside. I still remember how, tense, furious, I climbed to the cockpit. Sat down. On the left-hand seat. My seat. Shaking. Yes. Heavy-hearted. With tears in my eyes. Of course. It all came back to me.

I still remember how the young civilian pilot who now had command of this plane stood behind me and asked, deeply affected, whether I was alright.
He didn't let anyone else into the plane. We sat together for a while, as though acclimatising ourselves to it.
My heart was heavy, so heavy.
And I remember how I began to talk, to tell him about it. Hesitantly, at first.
With long pauses. His hand on my shoulder. Telling him everything. All of it. Everything.

The photos on my desk. The warm light of my banker's lamp. The letter in my hands.
The empty wine glass.
My head crammed with images. I stand up again, go to the window and drink in the peace of the gloriously quiet country landscape in the snow.
I think of Helmut Berger, who, as a young German fighter pilot lieutenant, attacked the B-17 formation in a 190 and shot down several planes. Who was shot down himself during one of those surreal missions and, luckily, escaped with only minor injuries.

He wrote:

It was hell! I still wonder today how and why I survived those fathers and mothers who loved them, just as we had fathers and who loved us. They thought they were fighting for what was right; so did we. When we think back on the war now, we have to ask ourselves: why, for God's sake, did we have to shoot at each other?

There are still a few of these planes flying today, to my knowledge. B-17s, 25s, Messerschmitts, Mustangs, FW-190s, Kittyhawks, Spitfires, Junkers, Hurricanes, Lightnings, Typhoons, PBYs, Zeros, Dakotas...

I think of them as memorials.
Flying memorials, which need to be preserved.
Which can remind us of what lies beyond our fascination with their incredible mechanics.
Beyond the stunning, breathtaking feeling of flying.
Because they were Aviators too. Aviators.
On both sides.

They were Aviators.
Just like us.

Encounter

It happened last year. I really didn't expect it. It all began so innocently.

One of the friends I'd learned to fly with years and years ago had, even back then as an enthusiastic trainee pilot, dreamed of flying a biplane. A very specific type of biplane, with a specific engine and a specific appearance. He was totally obsessed with this plan; nobody could talk him out of it. He talked about it all the time, to everyone. He was really serious about it.

And, one day, it seemed he'd actually achieved it.

I'll never forget it: he rang me up in the middle of the night on a Friday. Was I free? He'd spoken to his bank earlier that day and had been calculating frantically ever since. The money would just about cover it, which he hadn't expected at all. He was home and dry!

I told him that he was completely mad, but nothing would dissuade him from jumping in his old Chevy and racing over to my place immediately.

Fine.

He leaned on the bell until I let him in, and we spent that dreary spring weekend occupied with beer, limp pizza that also served as breakfast after sleepless nights, litres of coffee, stacks of brochures, specialist journals, calculations, and phone calls, until, quite by accident, we stumbled across an inconspicuous little ad in an old aviation magazine.

We called the number immediately and arranged an appointment. The plane was still available. Incredible. The magazine was three months old.

It was also odd that the biplane - a gaudy blue Stearman - was apparently located at an airfield quite close to us, without us ever having heard of it before. We'd even landed there a few times and knew a couple of the local lads.

Incredible.

We decided not to drive there, but, as was only fitting, to fly. So a week later, on one of those spring afternoons hardly worthy of the name of spring, we hauled the Mooney from the hangar and took off.

I remember it perfectly. The weather was nothing to write home about: grey and overcast, with a low, broad ceiling of cloud and regular showers.

After half an hour, we reached the airfield: a perfectly ordinary little place with a solid runway, a strip of grass next to it for gliders, a few hangars, a filling station and the obligatory airfield bar.

As we slotted ourselves into the traffic circuit, I wondered again how I'd managed to miss this Stearman despite its being just forty miles from my home airfield. Such rarities were a major interest of mine, after all.

Strange.

Final approach. Instruments, no flags, gear down and three greens. Flaps as required, throttle as required, touch down and taxi out...

We parked the plane in the allotted position, and I climbed out over the wing and marched through the cool air to the air traffic controller's building to pay the landing fee. In the meantime, my friend attempted to find out where the Stearman was hiding.

We still had some time before our appointment, so we spent it loitering among the parked planes talking shop, and trying every trick we could think of to peek into a locked hangar where we suspected the biplane was housed.

Without success. Hm. Shame.

My friend danced about the place like a scalded cat. His impatience was infectious. Time crawled.

Then, glancing over at the car park by the bar, I saw an

enormous car pull up and a flashy, highly groomed man get out: tan, reflective black Ray-Bans despite the gloom, tie, perfectly cut A2 jacket, some rediculous fantasy patches on it, gold chain. Behind him in the car sat a blonde girl.

I watched as he disappeared into the tower. I would never in a million years have pegged him for the owner of a Stearman. My friend made a cutting comment about the difference between pilots and aviators, and we couldn't help but grin at each other, which meant we were all the more surprised when the man emerged from the tower shortly afterwards and headed straight for us. We stared at each other in disbelief.

A few seconds later, as we'd both tacitly feared, he introduced himself with astonishing politeness as the owner of the biplane, led us directly to the mysterious hangar we'd identified earlier, unlocked it and pushed open the rattling door himself.

There it was.

We walked around it, staring wide-eyed. It was beautiful. Together, the three of us removed the chocks and hauled the aircraft outside.

The biplane had been lovingly restored and was clearly in top condition. US registrated, not a single smudge of oil on the big Continental radial engine, expertly painted in the colours of a Marines training unit. For such an old aircraft, the cockpit was kitted out with every possible bit of high-tech gadgetry. Even the copilot's seat had more than just the usual set of dials.

Our eyes sparkled as we circled the plane curiously, moved the control surfaces and inspected the radial engine.

The dandified owner informed us that he'd bought the aircraft directly from a well-known restorer in Florida a few months ago, but that such an exposed style of flying was, as he put it, not comfortable enough. So he was selling it.

Okay then.

I watched my friend out of the corner of my eye.

As the pretty boy continued to talk entertaining nonsense, he walked around the biplane in his tatty flightsuit as though in a trance, eyes gleaming.

Would we be interested in a test flight? Stupid question.

We hauled the biplane over to the filling station. Nozzle in hand, I used a rickety ladder to clamber up to the top wing and fill the tanks to the brim.

My friend climbed almost cautiously into the cockpit. Pretty Boy took the seat behind him - though not before fumbling a white silk scarf into place around his neck with stilted nonchalance.

I had to make a serious effort not to burst out laughing.

I gave the *Prop clear* signal, the radial engine began to roar, and a few minutes later, the two of them snaked down the taxiway. I stood by the filling station and watched them go.

As the biplane thundered down the runway, engines rumbling, and climbed into the overcast sky, I was already on the way to the little bar for a hot coffee.

The drone of the radial engine faded gently into the distance. I could see through the window of the restaurant from quite a way off - and Pretty Boy's blonde companion was sitting at one of the lonely tables. As I got closer, I slowed in spite of myself.

139

That looked like… but that was impossible!

I opened the glass door a little hesitantly, went through the porch, and - without looking round at her - headed to the counter to wait for the barman.
Strange. I could have sworn that she looked just like Anke. How weird.
If I'm honest, it took me considerable effort not to turn around and look at her.
And, as it turned out, I didn't need to anyway.
It seemed she'd recognised me too: she called my name, clearly also a little uncertain.
I knew that voice well.
It was like being struck by lightning.

I was perhaps fourteen or fifteen years old. We were in the same class. Anke sat in the row in front of me, a little to the right. Almost all of my friends were infatuated with her.
Hardly surprising: she was, without question, the most beautiful girl we knew. Long, flaxen hair; slim and willowy in those tight jeans she always wore; incredible figure - we pretty much lost it when we saw her at the pool in a bikini. Plus, she was untouchably cool.
Just like the others, I was hopelessly in love with her, but in an idiosyncratic, romantic way - unlike my friends, who were always strutting around, propositioning her clumsily and trying to get the jump on one another.
They all failed; Anke was skilled in the art of the cool rejection.

Of course, I was much too shy to talk to her myself. If our eyes happened to meet during class, I more or less had a heart attack and spent the next few hours on cloud nine.

Of course, she didn't even notice.

Of course not.

I felt pretty stupid huddling against the counter. I could imagine what a pathetic sight it made:

me, the hardened pilot, sitting in a laughable little airfield bar in my ancient, crumpled green MA1, threadbare jeans and worn-out Chucks. Me, the guy with countless flight hours under his belt in every aircraft imaginable, Mr Cool himself, completely unflappable - sitting there almost too nervous to move, just because some girl had called his name.

Absolutely idiotic.

But I had to turn around. I had to.

I couldn't just stand there.

So, deep breath and time to fake it: turn slowly, then the expression of surprise - but for God's sake don't overdo it.

I still don't know whether I managed to make it look as cinematic as I intended.

My hunch had been correct - it really was her! Unbelievable! So I stood up and went over to her, feigning surprise.

Didn't I want to sit down? What was I doing here? How long it had been since we last saw each other! That kind of thing.

Her easy unselfconsciousness with me had my heart stuttering. Everything seemed to be breaking down again; the old emotions practically stunned me. I sat incredulously opposite her as she chattered cheerfully, witty and charming, entirely unperturbed; tossed her blonde mane over her shoulder with a flick of her hand; gave a radiant smile.

I was stuck in the past; all the idiotic ways I used to try to get close to her. Roaming around where I knew she'd be after school in order to run into her *totally by chance*; my friends' useless matchmaking attempts at basement parties they'd arranged themselves; a thousand unworkable plans for striking up a conversation; unsent letters; trips to the cinema that went south at the last second.

But once, I did in fact manage to take her to the airfield with me, and my friends were green with envy. I had just completed my first solo glider flights and wanted to impress her, but she was indifferent to everything I showed her; clearly bored by my explanations. She squinted into the sun, blasé, clearly dismissing it all as unimportant. She remained unimpressed even when, at the longed-for invitation of my flight instructor, I was permitted to grab a parachute and heroically prepare for takeoff in the front cockpit of the school's two-seater. Anke seemed to find other things more interesting, to the point of almost ignoring me. I took off and circled the airfield, but by the time I landed again, she'd simply up and left.

I was at my wit's end.

And the sweet ache that I both loved and hated that arose whenever I was near her, my daydreams, the bewildering new worlds that opened up in me when I thought of her...

And now I was sitting opposite her, making small talk over coffee with the memories swimming in my head, chatting innocently about old times - and yet I couldn't shake that familiar sense of insecurity.

Only when she repeated her offer of a cigarette did I manage to slowly shake off the fog of memories. Her smile hadn't changed a bit.

But for some reason, I seemed to be looking for trouble. I was curious, and somehow that calmed me. I just wanted to know how she felt, and I began to slip in vague references to the past just to see how she would react. She actually seemed interested; lost in thought: the good old days.

I kept needling away, restless; raked up the airfield story. She laughed until she nearly choked – thank goodness we're past that now, right? I forced a laugh too. Of course.

We kept talking, and I drew back instinctively, getting quieter. Anke stopped going along with my provocations, and finally I let it drop. Already a little more knowing.

When she went on, face glowing, to tell me about her *glamorous life* with Pretty Boy - the beach parties, the weekend trips to hip, exotic locations - and to bask in the reflected glory of her more or less fashionable celebrity friends, I finally gave up. I felt thoroughly shellshocked.

Anke seemed to notice, and gave the conversation another turn, working herself up over this stupid airfield we were stuck at and finishing by abusing the blameless barman.

By that point, her indignation was little more than background noise to me. I was staring almost dreamily out the window, watching the blue Stearman its descent on short final.

She noticed my gaze and, once again smiling charmingly, told me how glad she was that her companion was selling that

143

monster. Flying was uncomfortable enough to begin with, she said, and that *thing*, as she put it, made it totally unbearable.

As the biplane touched down and taxied on the grass runway outside, I had to pull myself together in order not to give vent to my anger and disappointment.
Instead of giving her a piece of my mind, I gestured at the plane outside, muttered an excuse and got up to go.
Nice to see you again, she said in parting, and that was the final straw for my self-control.
I slammed the door wordlessly behind me on the way out.

My friend, incidentally, bought the plane - for such a ridiculously low price that we initially thought there must be some kind of catch.
The log that came with the Stearman revealed that, besides the complete overhaul in Florida, it had also had a complete overhauled engine installed - only be running 40hrs SMOH. We couldn't believe it.
The evening the contract was signed, my friend showed up at my door again with a huge bottle of Moët & Chandon, which we promptly disposed of.

The whole thing had been a real stroke of luck.

It didn't take long for me to complete my rating for the Stearman. We often go flying together in it.
I have my own hangar key now, and my friend lends me the Stearman whenever I want to go up in it.
Flying it is like a dream. It's almost indescribable.

A real stroke of luck.

And sometimes, when I'm sitting alone in the plane with the wind from the propellers ruffling my hair, or racing playfully with the Boeing at low altitude, I can't help but think back on that encounter.
Anke, too, once rode in this wonderful plane.

And I decide that perhaps it's for the best if some wishes don't come true.

Others,
though...

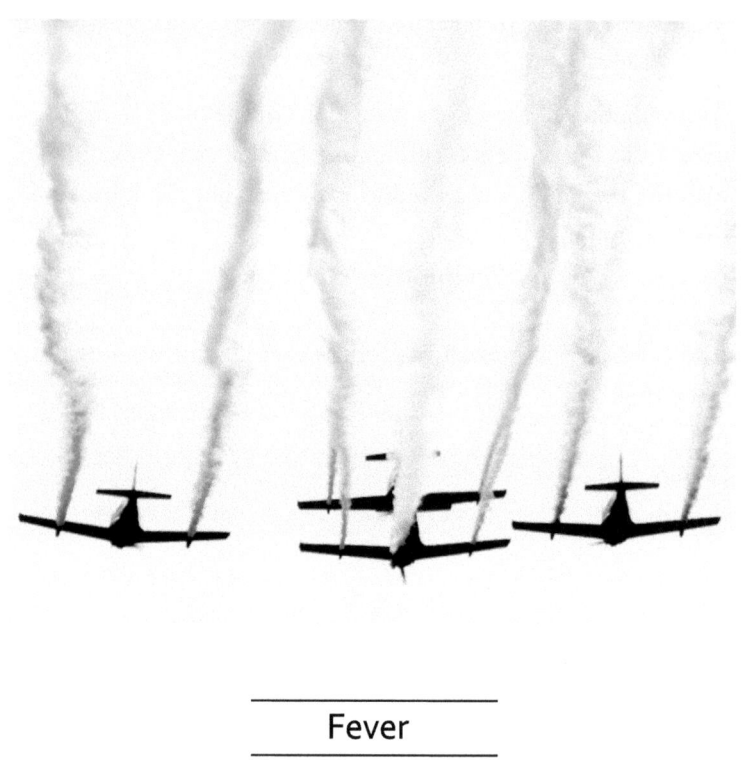

Fever

No ordinary Friday. I glance at the clock: **1300**. I've got the fever again. The season is here. Today's the first day. After the winter. After all the planning.
Restless and excited, I drive to the local station. I want to be off, to be there at last.

I board the crowded slow train, which saunters towards Hanover much too slowly for my tastes, stopping at every tree and post box along the way.
The familiar, homely landscape sways by slowly. I won't be

seeing it again for a while...

1440

I loiter impatiently among the other passengers on the noisy platform at Hanover, waiting for the arrival of my intercity express. Unchecked Friday crowds. I eye the people around me. Killing time.

Coke and dry pastries eaten standing up.

1453

Finally, I'm on the train. I find my compartment. Erratic, loud, edgy hustle and bustle all around me. Good thing I reserved a seat. I fish my laptop and a couple of aviation magazines out of my pilot's suitcase and order coffee. The train whisks calmly through northern Germany; onward, ever onward. And I feel myself slowly becoming calmer too.

But the fever is still there.

1613

Hamburg. I wind my way off the dirty grey train in a cluster of passengers. Inquiring glances. I hurry through the station with my things to the agreed meeting point.

Nobody there. Damn.

So I wait.

A new experience: I hear my name being called over the loudspeaker! And then again in English.

Frank is at the nearest counter; I see him waving from miles off. Sorry I'm late; couldn't find a parking space again. Never mind. Slaps on the back; warm looks.

We find our way to his car. There's a ticket on the window. Never mind. We shrug.

Frank races purposefully through Hamburg's after-work traffic at zero altitude (*there's no other way to do it here*). We leave the oppressive grey suburbs to the north of the city behind us and reach the airfield at Uetersen just half an hour later. Our parking space is directly in front of the hangar.

1700

The Do is still in the hangar, and we put our backs into hauling it out onto the grass. Frank does the external checks while I stow my gear in the compartment. Finally, he and his co-pilot (*Evenin', I'm Klaus*) clamber into the cockpit, complete their checks and fire up the engines. I make myself comfortable on one of the spartan cots to starboard, collect a headset from its hook and strap in.

We lumber across the field to the runway. Andy presses the throttle down; the engines roar; the Do 28 rattles over the turf, apparently devoid of any suspension; we take off swiftly; Andy swings the plane gently over the boundary and up in a beautiful broad rightwards curve.

1720

Looking down: the Außenalster Lake gleams, the port, the Köhlbrand Bridge. We thunder over Hamburg and, as ever, I'm glued to the window. Through the headset, I hear us bidding farewell to the control zone. Have a good flight, Do two-eight...

The weather is good: 3/8 scattered oktas of cover with a cloud base at almost 5000 feet. A few minutes later, the glittering Elbe vanishes behind us and we're enroute.

I gaze up front towards the cockpit. Frank turns around and beckons me with a nod of the head. His co-pilot switches places with me. I clamber into his seat, lock it in place and strap myself in. Frank grins. Want to take your Do rating while we're up here? I can only nod. I must be grinning like a Cheshire cat.

He quickly talks me through it all. I drink it in. One more glance at the map and the GPS, then I hear Your control! through the headset and take the beautiful old-fashioned yoke in my hands. I try a few gentle tilts of the control surfaces, test various power settings both clean and with flaps, feel my way around the stall speed, fly two full circles and then head back on course. Not bad. Pretty fun, this good old Do. I couldn't be happier. Yeah! That's the way to do it! I think.

1750

We're roaring cosily eastwards. I busy myself investigating the cockpit as Frank grins sceptically. We're navigating visually, working through the reference points and checking them using the GPS as we go. After a while, I spot Berlin abeam to port in the mist. We enter various courses, cobbling together a path between the airliners and through Charlie airspace. The weather gets noticeably worse; the cloud base falls considerably; we ask the controller for permission to go lower; I reduce the engine speed and we descend.

1815

The weather is getting lousier and lousier. We plod across the sky at less than 1000 feet; a light drizzle; the GPS promises us an ETA of twenty minutes. Frank waves his co-pilot forward; I clamber back to my cot but sit as close to the cockpit as possible.

1833

The rain is now raging around the cockpit windows; we're flying through a few low-hanging wisps of cloud; the chimneys of the power station are now at eye level and all three of us are struggling to spot the airfield in between the opaque drifts of rain.

Finally, Klaus spies the bright revolving beacon of the tower far away amidst the grey, and we receive our landing clearance. Direct approach. No traffic circuit. No traffic at the field, we hear in a laconic east German drawl as we make our final approach. Frank circles a finger by his temple, shaking his head.

1840

I jump down from the cabin door and, naturally, land feet first in a huge puddle and get soaked through.

The organiser and his wife, sheltering under a large umbrella, come running through the streaming rain to greet us. Good to have you here…

We unload our things from the Do, secure the plane and hurry into the crew tent. In the distance, through the veil of rain, I see the silhouettes of empennages from the rows of decommissioned MiG-21s.

1900

We sit over beer in the warm crew tent, soaked to the skin. Most of the other pilots made it here before the rain; the open planes are already in the old NPA hangars. A general clamour of voices.

I huddle into a corner, fish my battered phone from my helmet bag and call home: *Yes, safely landed, no problems at all.* The little one always asks: *Daddy, Daddy? Is she in bed? Is she sleeping? Good! Goodnight.*

Somehow it still gets to me every time, spending three days away like this...

2200

We're sitting with Freddy, Bea and Uwe, beginning to plan the next day. Weather report? Freddy brandishes his stack of fax paper and we bend over the surface weather maps. Looks good, should work out...

Mike from the depths of north Germany has arrived: Sodding traffic, I'm getting another beer or five. Laughter, cigarette smoke. Then the order: Let's go! We're off to the hotel. All our junk in the crew bus.

2400

The hotel bar. Familiar faces, more laughter. Come on, let's hit the sack, suggests someone, and we nod.

0104

We finally undress and throw ourselves into bed. Tomorrow will be a long day...

Next day

0500

The alarm's merciless pulsing scream tears me from sleep; I'm wide awake in an instant. The fever...

The first critical glances outside: 8/8 cloud cover at perhaps 400 feet; light rain. Great. And on the very first day! TV weather report: too imprecise. First, a shower.

0530

Breakfast. It had to be organised specially for us this early in the morning. The others trickle in, all still sleepy. Hot coffee and warm rolls reanimate us, and we go through the flight line again while we're there: we'll need to move some of the planes; it won't work like this.

Poring over the local papers: impressive announcements about the show. Weather checks: still mixed, but it should improve. Gulping down the last rolls; it's getting late...

0600

Our crew bus is already waiting by the hotel entrance, engine running. We hand over our pilot's suitcases, helmet bags and other belongings to be stowed somewhere in the luggage compartment. Someone yells, *Boarding completed!* The doors swish shut; the bus starts to move; we're off.

0630

A half hour drive through vast fields of crops; a few grey farmsteads along narrow, dilapidated roads. Looking out the windows is almost like travelling back in time.

The airfield.

A huge expanse.

We drive past the former guardhouse, the derelict barracks, sports halls, officers' messes. Among them, a decommissioned MiG-15 on a gigantic concrete plinth juts heroically into the overcast sky. Then the first hangars. The bus thunders across the gigantic apron. Here, too, everything is grey and drab. Most of the planes outside are still covered; the exhibitors' and retailers' stands behind the barriers still empty. Gigantic hangars, doors open wide. The semi-circular tower with the glass gallery.

A film set, I think to myself.

Silent as the grave.

We come to a halt by the crew tent at the far end of the ramp. A big mobile home next to it serves as a moveable office. The crew tent's kitchen team is already there. Their first official act: making coffee. Our first official acts: checking the barriers again; going through the list of planes and noting who needs to be moved where.

0700

Paperwork, briefing prep, copying lists for pilots, collecting together all the key paperwork for the day.

0730

A trip to the tower to say hello to the ATCs. We climb the sweeping old artificial stone steps. Peeling beige walls and railings; the smell of strong cleaning products.

A short conversation about NOTAMs, extra frequencies and taxi procedures. Then down one floor to the met office. The antiquated fax machine spits a never-ending stream of paper: weather maps at various flight levels, METAR and TAF codes, forecasts, large-scale weather patterns. We put our heads together sceptically. The general conclusion: things will improve; we just need to wait. Until we can see some kind of pattern in the clouds. At the moment, they're just a uniform grey slurry.

0800

The first ground crew briefing in our tent; we've finally finished the coffee. More than forty people have been assigned to jobs on the apron alone. Distributing walky-talkies, whose aircraft is whose, what needs special attention, when the breaks are, who's taking over from who when, where we need to keep an eye on the barriers, what the ID cards for today's event look like, where visiting aircraft should go, who's helping out at the filling station, how the sightseeing flights are being organised...

The flight line director's briefing, delivered with military precision; the crews tiredly slurping coffee and making notes. Following the display pilots' briefing, everyone gets a copy of the schedule for the morning programme. Any questions? The rampies head for the hardstandings. I fetch myself a third coffee.

0830

Racing along the apron in a car again; checking each aircraft as it reparks; giving the final instructions. Someone radios for us to head to the airfield entrance. There, the ticket desks are being set up and the car park attendants are already in place. The police are assisting with the traffic; the fire service, Red Cross and technical officers are on their way and want to know where they should set up. We send them to the crew tent. Hasty glances at our watches. Damn, we have to get back. But everything's under control here.

Nods, grins.

Hectic activity in the spectator area: retailers are putting up tents and opening stands and fast food vans.

0900

Briefing the pilots for the sightseeing flights; defining the take-off and landing areas. Overhead projection: airfield layout, taxiways, weather advisories, timings, traffic circuits, noise restriction zones. Paperwork: everything has to be recorded – preferably in septuplicate, on A4, in block caps, we joke. Pilot's licence numbers, aircraft data, insurance confirmations. The man from the responsible aviation authority is already there, sitting a little to one side and observing everything very intently.

Watches synchronised. Any questions? The pilots head to their planes; the man from the aviation authority greets us with a smile. It's all looking good; absolutely professional. Okay, then. Always nice to hear it from the experts, I think. I take a quick look at the sky. The rain has stopped and the first little specks of blue are starting to appear. And the first spectators, out there on the airfield...

0930

Someone presses another coffee into my hand; I've lost track of which one this is. We're sitting with the man from the aviation authority and our ATC, going over more paperwork: permissions, airfield documents, insurance, etc. etc. etc.

A short discussion of the schedule; everyone nods in agreement. Okay, good. That's how we'll do it.

Then talking through the plan for the morning programme with the briefing leader. Minor changes: we can't put the Spitfire on until the afternoon; it's only coming over from England this morning. Besides that, it's all good. Outside, aircraft engines begin to roar; the planes taxi out of the hangars towards the ramp. Soft music from the transmission system; the technicians are checking the settings. The first display pilots arrive in the crew tent. We wave our hellos to old acquaintances. My walky-talky beeps at me: a call from England. The Spitfire and the Corsair took off from Duxford fifteen minutes ago, heading for Germany. Estimated arrival time: in two hours and thirty minutes. I exhale and pass the message on to the others straightaway.

1000

Briefing for the morning programme - all in English. Schedule, more overhead projector slides. Weather advisories, airfield location maps. Traffic circuit, minimum heights and distances from the spectators, display line, emergency procedures, alternative airfields, radio procedures, information from air traffic control, start-up and taxi procedures, refuelling opportunities, start-up assistance - all reeled off professionally, interspersed with occasional questions. Start of the first schedule: **1130**. Watches synchronised. Any questions?

I'm standing way out to the front of the apron, looking over at the take-off runway, when someone behind me yells, *Hey, check six*! Seconds later, an almighty roar swallows me up: the Tornado from Eggebeck Air Base, thundering across the airfield at perhaps 200 feet on its afterburners. Midfield crossing. It greets us with a quick wing wave, reaches the other side of the airfield, climbs vertically until it touches the clouds, and slots itself into the traffic circuit for landing. A typical greeting ritual. The first rows of spectators at the barrier crane their necks to follow it.

1030
We sit down together again to discuss the final details. The team is working well; everything going like clockwork.
We check in with all the key posts via radio, getting a brief confirmation each time.

The rampies are hauling the first planes from the line-up at the barrier to their starting positions on the apron.

1100
Yet another phone call: the Spitfire pilot, from his stopover in Münster. The Spitfire and Corsair have refuelled and are ready to take off again.
Two T-6s taxi past outside; they'll be kicking off the programme in just a few minutes. Hundreds of spectators are still flooding into the site. I check my watch. It's almost time. I

hurry to the apron; a technician presses a radio mic into my hand; another glance at my watch... I greet the spectators at **1129**.

1130

The start-up clearance for the T-6 formation comes over the radio, and we're off: act after act soars above us, plane after plane takes off and wows the spectators with its programme. But I hardly have time to enjoy the show myself. Now and again, a Pitts performs an aerobatics routine set to music, and I can put the mic into my leg pocket and take a quick breather.

The event organiser races along the flight line on his scooter and pauses briefly next to me. *Everything okay? Got a sec?* I nod. He parks the scooter and sits down next to me for a couple of minutes. Time to start preparing the afternoon programme ... *Let's start with the Mustang, yeah?*

A police officer updates us over the service radio: hefty tailbacks at the entrance, but it's all under control. In the meantime, there's press to be done (*What kind of plane was that, then?*), new pilots arriving (*Where should we go and when's the briefing?*), a quick trip to the crew tent *(Any coffee left?)*, the organiser giving a TV interview in a corner (*And please look at the reporter, not the camera*), the constant crackle of radio traffic (*Got a couple of parents who've lost their kid; where should I send them?*), phone calls (*I'm Mr Big with a Cessna 172 from blah blah blah, can we land at your airfield?*), VIPs to be greeted (*The flight here was simply magical!*), stress stress stress.

Just so long as I'm still giving the moderation enough attention...

It's only when the MiG-29 roars upwards in an 80° afterburner take-off to close the morning programme that we're able to take ten minutes to check out the flight line ourselves, eyes gleaming.

1330

It's the lunch break, but there's no time for me to relax: I quickly grab something to eat in the crew tent before preparing the briefing and talking to the flight line director. The Spitfire and the Corsair landed a little while ago, so we head over to say hello. Then I have to discuss the afternoon programme with the man from the aviation authority. He's totally satisfied; praising how smoothly it's all going.

Well, what was he expecting?

1400

Briefing for the afternoon programme and debriefing following the morning's efforts. The air boss thanks the pilots for their neat work: ... *Nobody spoiled it, everything well-save, thanks a lot!* A brief round of applause. Then, just like at the morning briefing: schedule, overhead projector slides, weather advisories, airfield location maps, traffic circuit, safety clearances...

1430

The spectator areas are now full to bursting; visitors crowd up against the barriers and around the planes; we speed along the flight line in the car to check everything again; the afternoon programme will soon be underway. The ground crew are hard at work: the first planes are already in position out on the ramp. The display begins in fifteen minutes.

1500

Right on time, the P-51D Mustang takes off.

Countless cameras turn to follow it; the 40,000 spectators are entranced by the rich throb of the Merlin engine and the speed

and manoeuvrability of the old fighter plane. Then comes a
new source of stress: the mobile APU has had it and we need
to conjure a new one from somewhere. Meanwhile, a reporter
for an aviation magazine is asking whether he can go up in one
of the warbirds... and so on and so forth, almost worse than the
morning. By now, it's pretty hot. Up above, the pilots romp
through a bright blue sky. It's electrifying.

1800

Everything's gone smoothly, and now things are starting to
calm down a bit.

There are still plenty of visitors checking out the parked
aircraft, but the only ones still up there in the evening sky are
the sightseeing pilots buzzing around in their sports planes.

1830

Charlie comes up to me as I'm staring dreamily at the Corsair.
Whatcha doing now? he asks. I shrug, exhausted. *Probably going
for a beer,* I reply, and he shakes his head.
Come on, let's fly. We've got something up our sleeves, he says
significantly, gesturing to his Stearman. *Coming?*
Hmm? I drawl, and I jog after him, curious to see what he has
planned. Once I've strapped myself in and he's clambered into
the cockpit behind, he says, *We've put together an eight-ship to
take a spin over the city. Haven't got clearance, but let's just go for it,
yeah? You're the lead. You know this area, right?* I laugh loudly
and shake my head. He responds with a rumbling laugh: *Well,
great! I thought – I don't either! But hey, we'll manage!*
You're all crazy! I bawl over my shoulder.

We fire up the engines and taxi along the endless track towards
the runway in a gentle zigzag. A pack of biplanes is gathering
at the threshold: two Stearman, four Tiger Moths, the Pitts

Special and a Focke-Wulff Stieglitz. The controller gives us the go-ahead and we take off into the soft evening light. A broad leftwards curve sets us on course for the city to the west. The bright orange sun is already hovering over its outskirts. We form up into a wide V. The sunset sky is clear and bright as we drone above the city streets, way up high and visible for miles.

We change formation, and as I look around me at the cloud of biplanes in the last radiance of the sun, I feel a deep peace come over me.

I peel off my aviator hat and let the cool air, the breeze and the swell of sound from the engines wash over me. We wave to each other from the open cockpits; the slight bobbing and weaving of the formation is like a gentle dance; every now and again, the fixed wings blaze with balmy reflected light and the propellers look like huge blank discs; silhouetted against the low, dazzling light, our long string of planes cascades through the sky. We circle the city in a broad, gentle curve, engines rattling, heading into the vast red sun that's now just a hand's breadth above the horizon.

When we approach the airfield again in the faint evening light and radio for landing clearance, we're told to delay: *Stay well clear of pattern, Transall for high-speed low-go on long final, afterwards for landing. Formation establish as number two behind, use caution on wake turbulence, stand by for landing clearance – acknowledge.*

So we stay where we are. Charlie banks and we watch from

above as the big C-160 shoots along the runway at zero altitude, almost sticking to the concrete, before pulling up sharply at the end of the track. Ten minutes later, we've touched down too. It's nearly dark.

2000

Nobody left in the crew tent, but the Transall's ramp is down, and inside, there's a regular pub atmosphere. A clamour of voices. I push my way forward to the cockpit and am immediately handed a beer. An old crew; I know them from last year. I'm handed from person to person until I reach the co-pilot's seat at the front. We spend a long time chatting; hoots and yells drifting from the cargo bay behind us.

It's been a successful first day; everyone's pleased; great atmosphere.

The crew bus takes us back around **2400**.
Another half hour at the hotel bar...

Final day

We've made it through two and a half days of the air show. Two days of constant stress. Two days full of aircraft. Two days full of events. Like a fever dream. Countless planes and countless take-offs. Several litres of coffee. Beer. Reminiscences with various friends.

And three fantastic flights: that incredible sunset biplane trip, then a wake-up call over the city and the surrounding area with the B-25 the next morning. The Mitchell thundered into the crystal-clear morning sky on more than 3000 HP, with a special take-off clearance. We swooped low over the city and the broad fields, plunged into a long forest clearing and overtook an intercity train as we sped above a railway line. The cockpit speed indicator hovered just under 230 knots.

And then in the evening, we take the Yak-52 and flip it upside down: a gallant adventure of rolls, loops, turns, Cuban eights and knife-edge interludes against the peaceful evening sky. It's nearly dark by the time we pull up out of the final low flyover and shoot up almost vertically into the endless dark blue expanse above us. After another half Cuban eight, we drop all the flaps and wheels. We land and taxi over to refuel.

I sit out on one of the wings and let the breeze from the propeller wash over me.

It's almost **1900**.

The retailers have dismantled their stalls; stewards are busy stacking the barriers; the biplane formation vanished over the horizon half an hour ago.

I sit on my pilot's suitcase, waiting for the shuttle to the railway station.

Tired. Exhausted.

Filled with wonderful experiences, long conversations, rare aircraft, surprising flights.

Important friendships.

The air show family.

Later - much later - that night, as the slow train drops me back in my little town and I grope my way to my car, all I can think about is getting a few hours' sleep.

Sleep, sleep. Sleep.

I sit behind the wheel for a few moments, exhausted, before starting the car and mulling it all over.

I smile slightly as I reflect that I'll be back here again by midday just two weeks later.
At this station.
On the way to some big former military airfield somewhere in the south. I smile slightly as I visualise myself restless and excited once again. Ready for the next air show.

The fever will be back.

Last Call

M an, I'll remember the day I met Clarke forever. It happened like this: one summer, an old friend who flew Learjets for a VIP carrier had a bunch of assignments in the south of Spain. I had plenty of time on my hands, and, after a couple of phone calls, he took me with him on one of his trips down south with an empty plane - without permission, of course. I'd heard about an air show at Morón Airbase to the south-east of Seville, and he promised to make a spontaneous stopover and drop me off there.

So I amused myself with the leftover smoked salmon and champagne, trotting between the cockpit and the leather sofa in the back as we cruised to Spain at FL300.

We landed and parked in the air base's VIP spot, and I clambered happily down from the air-conditioned Lear into the blazing southern heat as my friend kept the engines running.

I helped to fold up the little gangway and watched as he shot along the runway a few minutes later, climbed sharply, and quickly vanished, a tiny speck in the bright blue sky.

The flight line was well provisioned with Spanish, American and British military jets. Off to the side were the Patrulla Águila's seven CASA C-101s; behind them the transporters, helicopters and scouts; in between, a few warbirds from the Second World War; right at the back of the ramp, shimmering with heat haze, I could make out two C-5s and a few KC-135s.

I saw Clarke for the first time right after he landed. In tight formation with a Spitfire, his Hurricane hurtled over the burnt, yellow-brown strip of grass separating runway and apron, belly nearly touching the ground. They pulled up, and the Spit performed a military grade standard overhead break and slotted itself into the traffic circuit behind the Hurricane.

Soon after, the two of them had touched down neatly one after the other and taxied to their parking positions.

Clarke hauled himself confidently out of his Hurricane, scrambled onto the wing, leapt lightly down to the ramp and started chatting to the Spitfire pilot, laughing loudly. He was on the short side and a little stout; he wore Randolph sunglasses and a faded green American flight suit without any insignia.

But the really striking thing about him was his magnificent head of red hair, which was visible for miles around.

The paintjob on the two planes was somewhat megalomaniacal, as Clarke later admitted: his Hurricane Mk. I bore the colours of Douglas Bader during his time as squadron leader of the No. 242 Squadron. I still remember the blue squadron insignia resplendent beneath Clarke's cockpit on the port side.

Will's Spitfire was a Mk. IX, done up to resemble that of *Johnnie* James Edgar Johnson, a British fighter ace who fought in the Battle of Britain and used the call sign *Juliet-Echo-Juliet*. Later, when I asked Clarke whether this wasn't laying it on a bit thick, he just laughed and said, *Ya know, kid, the Brits love this!*

The air show programme was great and we enjoyed ourselves despite the blazing heat up above the Andalusian plain. I still don't know how I ended up on the guest list for that evening's party.

Really, I have no idea.

They'd built a kind of stage in a large hangar and parked a freshly polished F-16 on either side as decoration. Four or five long rows of beer tent benches, an open space in front of the stage with a dance band tuning up, a long bar to the left, and clouds of the obligatory parachute decorations hanging from the ceiling. The heavy hangar doors only open a crack.

Things didn't really get started till it was almost dark. The dance floor was packed; the band dispassionately blaring some kind of pop crap; the tables by the bar crammed with people in flight suits: pilots from both the base and the air show.

On the other side - and clearly separate from them - sat the usual figures in suits and dress uniforms, with equally dolled up women on their arms. In the middle of the crowd of flight suits, I spotted Clarke's red hair. I couldn't help but chuckle. Who was that? I wondered.

We met again at the bar. I'd decided to order something at last and had just worked my way painstakingly up to the counter when he shoved through the crowd with cheerful energy, yelling *Hey hey, anything to drink around here?* Then he was next to me, and the only thing I could do was to press the first available beer into his hand. He took it with a beaming smile and a *Thanks kid, c'mon, we're gonna get this*, and then, before I knew what was happening, he was tugging me over to the table where he'd taken up residence. Thankfully I'd already managed to grab a second beer.

We chatted for a little while and, without further ado, he introduced me laughingly to William - Will - who I recognised as the Spitfire pilot. Will was a wiry, robust man with a very dry sense of humour; the exact opposite of Clarke, who later told me that they'd known each other forever and had flown together in the RAF. Clarke went on to dub me *the bloody German*, but he always laughed as he said it, so I never took it badly. I knew what he meant.

That night in Andalusia, Clarke stood up, gestured to me and bellowed, *Folks, you need to know this kid, 'cause he knows how to get the drinks in here!* And that was more or less it for the evening - or the night. After that, he always called me *kid*. I got used to it after a while.

I woke up the next morning in a barracks bed, wondering how I'd got there.

I still don't know the details, but it seems that Clarke had taken a liking to me and simply scooped me up and took me with him.

An army minibus drove us back to Morón that morning, and we ate in the officers' mess along with all the others. I hung out with Clarke and his friend for the whole day, flew with them in the Spitfire and the Hurricane, and let him explain the aircraft to me, patiently and full of curiosity. I'll never forget those two remarkable days.

So that was Clarke.

We befriended each other at that Spanish air base; swapped addresses, telephone numbers, emails.

That evening, my friend with the Learjet came roaring in to land again. I introduced everyone, but we were almost out of time - the slot for our return flight was coming up fast.

We said our goodbyes in the midst of the bustle and, after an impressively low flyover, we put the Lear's turbofans to work and ascended to FL340. Around two and a half hours later, we were back at our airfield in Germany.

I was dead tired, but overflowing with new experiences.

The first email from Clarke arrived just a few days later, and from then on, we wrote to each other a few times a week.

To begin with, he sent me his dates, as he called them: the days and locations of his appearances - whether alone or with Will - at various air shows, veterans' meetups and other events. He also praised or condemned hotels at length, reported on unusual aviation experiences and updated me on the other pilots that he met.

I told him about my - by comparison relatively insignificant - excursions, which nonetheless brought us together. He always asked for specific details, and he wanted to know everything about what I was doing. Everything. The airfields, the planes, my feelings, the weather, and I don't know what else. Everything. He liked the way I wrote, and we were both deeply grateful for the opportunity to fly and the incomparable experiences and sensations it offered us. That was another of the things that we wrote about a lot; sometimes very poetically. Naturally. I've still got all our conversations saved somewhere, of course.

Four or five times a year, we'd meet at some airfield somewhere in Europe and have a great time together.

And I don't just mean the usual drinking sessions - though of course there were some of those, too.

Clarke introduced me to dozens of interesting people. He was always at the heart of the aviation scene, and sometimes wrote reports and articles for pilots' magazines.

Oddly enough, he always seemed amazed whenever this happened. I always had to send him the magazines, links or articles immediately - assuming he hadn't managed to find them himself already. It always bewildered me a bit, but I was also a little proud.

And Clarke always knew how to surprise me with the help of his vast network of contacts. One spring, I almost fell out of my chair when he informed me, almost by the by, that he'd found a space for me in a C-47 flying over the Channel from Devon to take part in the D-Day commemoration events on the Normandy coast. But that's another story...

He was constantly arranging these madcap schemes, and was always delighted to witness my surprise at them. In no time at all, we were fast friends. Of course, flying meant everything to us, and I soon knew the whole history of his Hurricane with all its ins and outs, while he - as far as I know - knew my flight log off by heart, along with every story I told him about my trips. But that wasn't all that the friendship was based on.
Sure, we were used to downing pints together and merrily tearing each other to pieces. I've never met anyone who could take so much abuse as Clarke and still come down to breakfast the next morning so cheerfully undaunted. But we always looked out for each other. Always.

After just a few years, we knew each other extremely well. If one of us had something on our mind, we could stay up the whole night talking to each other on the phone - it was totally normal for us. I always welcomed Clarke's thoughtful, discerning advice, and I often succeeded in soothing him when he got himself worked up or took something too much to heart. Our discussions were intense, but our opinions rarely differed that much. And we hardly ever got the chance to fly together in the same plane.
Clarke's pilot's intuition and experience were simply stunning,

and they were further animated by his innate ability and lightness of touch. When I asked him about other pilots who always did everything by the book and without a trace of humour, he just shook his head in incomprehension and grinned. *Uptight idiots, kid. They don't really fly. Forget it.*
So we flew around Europe, taking turns to tell tall tales, just like old friends driving a well-known stretch of motorway together. But Clarke didn't miss a thing, even on familiar routes. He always flew with an inner intuition that I still can't explain - even as a co-pilot. Sometimes he continued our conversations while on the radio, winking at me with Irish humour. This resulted in baffled queries from the controllers, which never failed to amuse us.

Even with countless flight hours under his belt, Clarke remained amazed by the beauty of cloud formations, by fields and rivers, by the broad landscapes unrolling beneath us. *Woooow, kid, take a look at this*, he would say, leaning forward and pointing something out to me, oblivious to everything else. And I felt - and still feel - the exact same way.

And Clarke's unbelievable sense of mischief never faltered. I remember the approach to a sleepy amateur airfield somewhere close to the Ruhr. We were in an old V35 Bonanza that I was planning to fly back down south. We wanted to refuel first, and the AIP said that the local air traffic control spoke English. Clarke grinned broadly at me, tapped the approach chart and said, *Hey kid, let's check this out*, before addressing the ATC in English.
The response came in the same language, but a shaky, laboured

version that served as all the encouragement Clarke, now feeling his oats, needed. We entered a downwind approach and, in a broad Irish accent and at impressive speed, he requested *permission for a low-go, high-speed simulated low-level tower attack, afterwards full stop.*

A considerable pause followed as the bewildered ATC attempted to decipher this unusual and, to him, almost unintelligible request. At last, the radio crackled with an uncertain *Yes, Sir,* as he attempted to avoid losing face. Clarke grinned broadly at me once more, gave an exaggerated sidelong glance at the airspace and pressed every lever firmly down.

We thundered past the tower at more than 170 knots, just an arm's length away from the control tower. Clarke sent the Bonanza into a screaming ascent, turned sharply to the left, overbanking slightly, and, once our speed had slackened, dropped all the flaps and wheels. Half a minute later, he flew across the threshold at perhaps 150 feet on a Sarajevo approach, plummeted almost vertically down towards the runway, flared briefly at minimal speed, touched down as gently as you like, and taxied to a standstill. And all from the co-pilot's seat. He called it a *Hollywood approach.*

As we taxied past the fence, a few lonely Sunday spectators waved to us. I saw a couple of them applauding.

Just the way Clarke liked it.

Luckily the ATC had a sense of humour, and once Clarke had slapped him cheerfully on the shoulder and bellowed, *Pleased to meet ya, mate,* there wasn't much more he could do about it.

We fell apart laughing.

It was a very rare and very special friendship. Unique. Truly. I could trust him with anything and he could - I believe - do the same with me.

Then something changed.
Radically.
It happened fourteen years ago.
In the middle of the summer. August.
A glorious summer.
I had met up with Clarke and Will in Holland just a few days ago, and, as ever, we'd had a whale of a time. Clarke told me that they planned to fly to Italy again in the next couple of days for an air show at a military airfield near Venice. I didn't pay much attention at the time; this was business as usual.
But then, late one evening, I heard the phone ring. I was sitting in front of my laptop with a cold beer, tinkering with an article I'd started. A friend from my home airfield was calling.
Had I seen the news?
I immediately assumed the worst and scrambled to the TV, phone still in hand, to find a news programme - any news programme.

Will's Spitfire had crashed in Istrana. Fire, pilot dead almost on impact, no chance of survival.
I flipped through the channels. Images taken from a helicopter: the smouldering wreck of the Spitfire in the middle of a runway. At the end of the concrete strip, on a taxiway in front of a shelter, stood Clarke's Hurricane.

Parked, and clearly undamaged.

I hastily fumbled for my mobile and immediately called Clarke, but all I got was his voicemail. I left a brief message, begging him to call me back.
Needless to say, I was seriously concerned about him. Of course I was shocked by Will's crash, but there was nothing to be done about that now, as strange as that sounds.
I knew that he was one of Clarke's best friends, but I didn't know him as well as I did Clarke.

I was shell-shocked.
I had seen accidents like this in person before, and it still sends an icy shiver down my spine to think of them.
Especially when I know how good the pilots involved were. Pilots like Will. I couldn't explain it.

And the news reports were already full of self-proclaimed experts throwing around crude theories about the crash. He must have. He could have. He should have. What if he'd–?
Only one thing seemed to be certain: the accident didn't happen during the flight, but as the Spitfire came in to land on the 08 in Istrana.

Of course, I too immediately began to look for explanations. And, of course, I didn't find any, though I quickly rattled through all the facts at my disposal. A huge military airfield with a long runway suitable for jets - no shortage of space. Sure, the Spitfire's narrow landing gear is perfect for grass, but touching down on a concrete runway is far from unusual, and shouldn't be a problem for anyone who knows what to watch out for. Any tailwheel pilot in a Cub would know that. I'd discussed it with Will himself often enough. He knew what to do in that situation. And even if he'd lost control of the Spitfire after landing, with the wheels down, the accident would have looked different from what I'd seen on the TV.

I couldn't explain it.

Then my mobile rang. Clarke.

He was beside himself. I'd never heard him like this before. I barely recognised his voice: he spoke haltingly, with long, almost fearful pauses. He was okay, he said, but it was his fault. He couldn't talk now; he'd call me back later. And he hung up.

He'd never been so unforthcoming before. Even in serious situations, he could always give a precise, patient, judicious and exhaustive account of events.

It was a real shock. I knew immediately that something wasn't right. I had to get to him, as soon as possible.

I phoned around like a madman, chartered a Cessna 175 and, after an uneasy and almost sleepless night, flew down to Italy first thing the next morning. I had to land at the neighbouring airfield in Treviso, as the military airfield was once again closed to civilian aircraft. It was almost noon. I found someone with a car who could take me to Istrana, and went to the air base guardhouse to ask for Clarke.

It was slow going: I had to explain what I was even doing there in the first place, and the sentries were as stubborn as anything. Annoyed, I tried calling Clarke's mobile again; left another message. Arguing with the sentries was like banging my head against a brick wall. I stayed near the guardhouse, looking through the gate at the gate guards: an Aermacchi, and, behind it, an F-104 and a G-91. I paced uneasily around the car park in front of the guardhouse in the blazing heat. Before long, I knew the number and dimensions of the parking spaces by heart.

But then, barely an hour later, a solider waved me over. He only spoke broken English, but, after the usual tedious paperwork, he found me a car and drove me through the base, past a pair of old Thunderstreaks parked in the grass. Shortly afterwards, we stopped and got out by a flat building. The solider accompanied me through a couple of corridors leading out into the open air. I opened the glass door and there, a little way away, was Clarke, sitting under a sunshade by a pool.
Or, more accurately, slumped in a chair under a sunshade with a bottle in his hand.
I went over to him, thanking the solider, who continued to observe us from a discreet distance.
This wasn't the Clarke I knew. He was unspeakably miserable. When he saw me approaching, he wearily raised his head and nodded silently to himself for a moment. It's good to see ya, kid, he said, and began to cry, uncontrollably and at great length.

I sat down on the grass next to him and stayed quiet. He was silent for a long time. Now and again, he took a long pull from the bottle - whiskey.
Then he looked at me, shattered, and began to speak. He must have been drunk, but he spoke quietly and with great focus.
I tried to put questions to him calmly, and, haltingly, Clarke explained what had happened. Normally, the two of them took a break after the display and landed together: one after the

other with the usual safety distance between them, the Spitfire first. However, that morning at the briefing, they'd decided to add in another solo low-go with the Spitfire. Clarke would split off from the formation, merge into the traffic circuit and land first. The Spitfire would stay in a holding pattern until he had taxied away, and then come in for the flyover from the long final leg. At about 220 miles per hour, at 100 feet. This manoeuvre carried no risk: there were no issues on approach or on the ground, and the barriers that held back the spectators were significantly further away than they needed to be. No risk. None.

So Clarke landed and the Spitfire stayed in a holding pattern, waiting for clearance. Once Clarke had taxied the Hurricane to its parking position in front of a concrete shelter, the Spitfire came swooping low over the runway from the long final leg again, slotted itself into the traffic circuit, lowered its wheels as normal and - as normal - began its final approach. Clarke had just powered down the engine, he said, and he turned halfway around to watch Will's landing.
I knew that instinctive vigilance of his well: he was always alert, even if it didn't seem like it.
He paused, staring at his bottle. His eyes filled with tears again.

Over the first third of the runway, just before the flare, the Spitfire suddenly flipped as though seized by an invisible hand, and crashed into the concrete. It went up in flames almost immediately - the main fuel tank is located in front of the cockpit, right behind the engine firewall. The firefighters and rescue team were at the scene in an instant and pulled a severely

burned Will from the cockpit. He died on the apron. Clarke
was with him.

Shaking his head violently, Clarke interrupted himself again
and again with *It's all my fault, kid*. I wondered what could have
happened to make him think that, and tried to soothe him, but
he was convinced that the accident was his fault.
Nothing I said could persuade him otherwise. He cried again,
for a long, long time.
I sat beside him, stunned and distraught, for hours.
It was beyond description.
Beneath a radiant blue sky, in the glaring Italian sun, by a neat
pool on an air force base.
Insane.

In an attempt to tackle the situation, I began sorting out how
Clarke would get home. He couldn't fly on his own any more. I
tracked down an officer who spoke good English and, after
several phone calls, we managed to find a space for the
Hurricane in an empty shelter and a room for me on the base.
I handled Clarke's paperwork as best I could. He trotted
passively after me for the whole afternoon as though
unconscious of his surroundings, barely speaking.
That evening, we hauled the Hurricane into the hangar. With a
few minutes to myself, I drifted down the ramp and stared at
the runway, trying to imagine it, playing it back again and again.
Looking for mistakes.

It must have been very hot, I thought, like today. Hardly even a
breeze. Will and I had often discussed what to pay attention to

when landing the Spit: 85 miles per hour for the approach, keep the speed up until you're over the threshold - it stalls at 65 miles per hour - then, just before you touch down, pull the stick carefully and delicately towards you and cut the speed as quickly as possible. *On grass, she'll just taxi straight down*, Will always said. *On concrete, you need to keep a careful hold on the rudder and be gentle with the brakes.* And then he would laugh, scratch his moustache and say, *This is no witchcraft, kid. It's just another aircraft. That's all.*

I still couldn't believe it. It couldn't really be true.

And then, with a start, I remembered Clarke and hurried back. He was standing next to his Hurricane, shattered, staring blankly. At the officers' club that night, he got so drunk that it took three people to carry him back to his room. He kept repeating, *It's all my fault, kid, believe me*, and his gaze was fixed on mine as though I might be in a position to understand and forgive everything. He believed he'd caused the accident by changing the display programme; I understood that much. Of course, that was nonsense, but he couldn't let go of the idea and nothing I said could dissuade him.

The next day, I stuffed Clarke's few possessions into the Cessna, uneasily completed the remaining formalities, and assured some persistent bureaucrat that Clarke would make himself available for further questioning at the time specified. I called a friend of Clarke's in England who was prepared to pick him up from the airfield and take care of him. Then we flew over the Alps, made two brief stops in Germany to refuel, and crossed the Channel, heading for North Weald.

The weather was glorious.

Clarke barely spoke a word during the long flight; he just stared numbly through the window. He seemed drained of all his former passion and alertness.

So I set him down in North Weald, his friend collected him directly from the aircraft and I flew back to Germany, deep in thought.

A little later, through several not entirely legal channels, I managed to get my hands on the official accident report before it was published. It described the probable cause of the accident.

There were no technical issues; the Spitfire was in perfect technical condition. And there were no problems with the way the air show was run: all the rules were followed to the letter. All of them. According to the report, the accident was probably caused by an error of judgement on the part of the pilot. The authors suspected that, shortly before touchdown, the plane had flown through the wake vortices it itself had created during the previous flyover. Due to the plane's low landing speed, one wing stalled instantly. This caused an abrupt, irreversible movement in the wake vortex, which immediately flipped the aircraft over on its longitudinal axis. As a result of the density altitude produced by the very hot, stable high-pressure weather and the lack of wind, the unusually large wake vortices created by the first flyover would have remained above the runway for longer than usual, and could be assumed to be the cause of the accident.

And with that, the authorities declared the case closed.

I thought it over. Then I printed everything out, and, a few days later, took a commercial flight to England, rented a car at Stanstead, and drove to Clarke's house. A friend of his had flown the Hurricane back; I saw it in the hangar when I stopped at the North Weald airfield to ask after Clarke.
It seemed that no-one had seen him for weeks, so I drove to his flat. Clarke had always travelled a lot, but when I arrived at his little house in the suburbs of North Weald, his car was standing outside. I rang the doorbell and, a little while later, he opened the door; dressed in a tracksuit with his hair tousled. He seemed agitated, and his gaze was restless and fractured as he invited me in. *Good to see ya, kid,* he said quietly. *Let's have a drink.*

Clarke's flat was - as usual - pretty messy. We sat down in the kitchen. Clarke looked tired as he fetched a bottle and a couple of glasses from the cupboard. I took the accident report out of my bag.
He read it attentively, then swept the papers slowly aside. *It wasn't your fault; it was nobody's fault,* I said, but he just shook his head reluctantly and sluggishly explained that he should have realised; he should never have agreed to change the display programme. He'd always looked out for Will. Always.

I stayed the night.
He talked about Will.
About his funeral.
About their time together in the RAF; their training. They

181

started out in the Air Cadets together. Will's parents had died when he was still young: a plane crash in Asia. Will was very intelligent and very reserved, whereas Clarke was impulsive and always full of crazy ideas that kept getting him into trouble with his superiors. They'd definitely have thrown him out of the RAF if he wasn't such a good pilot - and if Will, who ranked higher, hadn't continually defended him.

Clarke laughed softly.

Will had always helped him; always made sure he scraped through their exams. And Clarke was there for Will whenever he got himself into a tricky situation, or when his reserve led him astray or caused him to miss an opportunity.

They flew the first Lightnings in the RAF, and then, later on, F-4s - sometimes even in the same squadron. They went halfway around the world together - flying, flying, flying, whenever they could.

Clarke also told me about his first flights in old warbirds and how, shortly before the end of his term of service, he passed the passion on to Will. Their first air shows in old Tiger Moths and Jennys, T6s, decommissioned Chipmunks and Provosts.

Their coup was the P-51 rating. Or at least, that's how he told it. And when, many years ago, they got the chance to buy the Spitfire and the Hurricane, they jumped on it immediately, putting all of their money plus some credit into the aircraft. They barely had enough left over to put petrol in their cars or go out for a meal once in a while, said Clarke. Those old bangers are priceless now, he said, and a faint gleam entered his eyes, but it ebbed away again just as quickly.

At first, they only flew within Britain, but soon they were in demand all over Europe. They didn't earn money from it.

Instead, they flew freelance charter jobs in their spare time. I remember asking Will about it once, and his shrugging reply: *The amount you get for air show work is hardly enough to preserve these birds.*

But they did fly. Word got around, and Will and Clarke's experience was soon in high demand: consulting gigs, film work abroad, this and that.

They perfected their displays with the military precision they'd learned in their youth – as precise, calculated and risk-free as possible. But the passion that went into every manoeuvre was breathtaking, as I well knew. *It's real fun, but it's not easy,* Will would always say deliberately when I praised him extravagantly following one of their displays.

Clarke was now in full flow: his narration might be slow, halting and accompanied by vast quantities of bourbon, but there was no stopping him. On and on.
Not for my benefit, but as though he needed to recapture it all somehow.

During the winter season, they did almost all the maintenance on their planes themselves. What they didn't know, they learned from old manuals or found veterans to help with. In the process, and more or less as an afterthought, they completed half a university degree in aeroplane engineering. They even got stuck into the Merlin engines themselves, only enlisting specialists to help when they were really at their wits' end.
I was well aware that Clarke knew everything there was to know about his Hurricane. Everything. He once showed me the

right way to stitch up the fabric of the control surfaces.

I was gobsmacked.

We never had any accidents, Clarke kept repeating. Never. I slowly began to grasp why he thought Will's death had been his fault, even if that was total nonsense. I was starting to understand.

What are you going to do now, Clarke? I asked.

He stared into his glass for a long time before he answered.

Dunno, kid. It's all gone, was all that he said - sad, suddenly devastated by his own words.

And then he carried on talking, and talking, and talking. It was early morning by the time we fell asleep, dead drunk.

I woke up on the sofa at noon, feeling pretty wrecked.

Clarke, still asleep, had remained hunched in his armchair.

I gently covered him with a blanket and made some hot coffee.

As I drove back, everything I'd learned that evening went round and round my head in an endless loop.

I felt as though I'd swallowed a stone and it had stuck in my throat. I didn't want to understand what had happened.

Clarke was an experienced fighter pilot.

An experienced warbird pilot.

He'd lived through God knows what.

He was always cheerful; he never let anyone get him down.

I didn't know what to think, but I was seriously worried.

I flew home a few days later, still unsettled and uncertain. I should have taken him with me. Damn it. I couldn't tell anyone else what had happened, either. They would have just shaken their heads. When my mates asked me about Clarke, I avoided or deflected the questions. But I stayed in touch with him. He still wrote to me, though all his former optimism was now gone. Our phone conversations were long and full of pauses. Long pauses. Sorrow. I simply listened to him. Sometimes the whole night long. He wasn't doing well. He wasn't doing well at all. As though he couldn't escape this burden he'd taken on.

I often doubted myself during this period.
But what in God's name could I have done? What? I couldn't tell him, *Come on, man, you need to move on; you're making a fool of yourself.* I couldn't tell him, Just get on with it and things will improve. I really couldn't just fob him off with some superficial, idiotic platitude. So I listened, and I wrote my heart out.

The months went slowly by and the grey, dreary autumn turned to winter. Clarke's emails became shorter and more resigned; he rang less often. When I called him, I felt like a father calling a child incapable of independent action.
Christmas came, and then the new year. It was a rough time. I often thought about Will and Clarke, and I ended up crying more than once.
What a death like that does to us. How a loss like that changes us. How it can rob us of all our courage. How corrosive it is; how it denies us everything and gives us nothing. How it leaves us facing a harsh hopelessness that can only be overcome by the light of our transfigured memories. How it overwhelms and obstructs us with self-pity. And closes off every avenue of escape.
I would never have believed it.

Slowly, I began to understand Clarke - better than I really wanted to.

Through unofficial channels, I discovered that the Hurricane had been sitting covered in the hangar in North Weald for several months, silent and untouched. Time passed.
My concern didn't.

It was mid-May when I received a call that roused me to action: one of Clarke's friends had dug up my number from God knows where and hauled me out of bed in the middle of the night. Clarke wasn't letting anyone into his flat anymore; nobody had seen him for weeks. I knew him so well, etc., etc. Did I have any idea what to do?
I immediately packed my things and bought a cheap ticket for an early morning flight to England on some budget airplane. There was no response when I rang Clarke's doorbell. I knocked, then pounded on the door. It was no use.
No reaction from inside; nothing at all. But there was a light on. Suddenly, I started to panic. I stopped caring about appearances. Before I could think about it, I broke a window, opened the latch and climbed into the flat. It was chaos: piles of slimy dishes, unidentifiable bottles, laundry, upset furniture, everything lying around at random. It stank.
I found Clarke in the bathroom. He was dead drunk and totally filthy; he barely recognised me, and it seemed to me as though he'd aged twenty years in just a few months. He was a truly pitiful sight.
I simply couldn't believe it. So I dragged him under the shower there and then, and then put him to bed - after I remade it with

the fresh sheets I'd managed to find somewhere. When I was sure that he was sleeping, I put the flat back together as best I could.

The next morning, I brought him breakfast in bed, but he refused to eat it. He could hardly speak; kept demanding bourbon; his gaze was unfocused; he was unshaven and seemed to have let himself go completely. To have been drifting along on his own resources, alone.
Clarke.
My friend.
Fighter pilot and air show ace.

Things couldn't go on like this. I pulled myself together forcefully. Very forcefully. We didn't have time for anything else. I called a doctor, who crammed him full of all kinds of medication, and begged one of his mates from the airfield for assistance so aggressively and at such length that he had no choice but to give in. He swore on his life that he'd check in on Clarke every day and call me immediately if anything changed. After all, there was no-one else to look after him.

What to do now? I had no idea.
But then, on the flight back to Germany, a crazy idea came to me out of the blue.
The very next day, I meticulously set about planning it. As far as I could see, it was our only hope.
No, I was certain: it was our only hope.
Sometimes, you just get a feeling: this is what you need to do. Exactly this and nothing else. It'll work, no doubt about it.

And - thankfully - it did.

So here's what happened.

Some background: a few years previously, a Dutch acquaintance of mine had acquired an old T-28D from France. He'd sweated blood over the restoration, and now flew it around in the colours of a US unit from the Vietnam War. I'd always been very impressed by this plane, so we got talking, and, one summer evening, we took a little trip in it together. Super cool. Soon after, he offered me the chance to take my rating in the 28. Of course, I was beside myself with excitement and immediately accepted. The T-28 might not have been a real warbird, but the D model with the Wright 1820 engine could get up some serious speed, tearing impressively through the sky. The cockpit was the size of a bathtub and incredibly comfortable, and the view out front through the canopy was similar to that of a fighter. So I flew my checkride, thundering around happily in the heavy machine. The old trainer was pretty placid and easy to fly. At the end, it came down on its tricycle landing gear like an overpowered, pregnant 172.

It was great fun.

And that had been that. Until now.

Suddenly, it seemed like the perfect solution. Sure, it would cost me a small fortune, but that was irrelevant. So I phoned Holland, and, after a bit of negotiation, booked the T-28 for half a week.

I prepared my plan down to the last detail and then, at the beginning of June, drove to Holland in the car. I flew a few loops of the airfield in the old bird for safety's sake, then took off for real the following day.

Over the Channel. To England.

Bang on schedule, with a life vest and all the other requisite bits and bobs.

The flight over the Channel is its own story: out over the water from Calais, the white cliffs of Dover on the misty horizon, tales of the Battle of Britain whirling in my head - it was spectacular.

I couldn't resist taking the opportunity to race along the south coast of Britain for a bit before heading back towards the mouth of the Thames.

I circled round far to the east of London, and, just three-quarters of an hour later, landed in North Weald.

The friend who was taking care of Clarke had helped me to reserve a space behind a hangar on some plausible pretext, out of sight of anyone in the tower. I'd checked it out thoroughly beforehand using photos and the approach chart.

So I taxied off the runway, requested my parking position and pulled up there. All according to plan.

A few days earlier, a friend had reported that Clarke was more or less back on his feet, though still unresponsive and fairly dependent on drink. Okay then.

I drove to Clarke's house. He still looked wretched. At least he was talking to me again: okay, only in short bursts and sometimes sounding pretty confused, but it was something.

That evening - with some effort - I succeeded in keeping him off the bottle. I cooked dinner for us and then sent him to bed. Early the next morning, I woke him, forced him - cursing all the while - under a lukewarm shower, and attempted a full

English breakfast.

Of course, he noticed that I was planning something.

What are you up to, kid? he kept asking. I gave him some story about an excursion; told him that he needed to get out of the house again. He shook his head. Never mind.

After breakfast, I shoved Clarke into the car and we drove out to the North Weald airfield. Of course, he knew the route, and he began to kick up a fuss, struggling and repeating, *Don't wanna go there, kid. Let's head home*, and so on. I simply ignored his mutterings.

I'd spoken to the people at the airfield in advance - at least, those who I didn't have to deliberately mislead - letting them in on my plan, so I was able to drive unchecked up to the hangar the T-28 was parked behind.

I got out and Clarke - as expected - stayed where he was, staring at the floor.

I knew it would be a challenge for him.

A serious challenge.

It was only when I aggressively demanded his help that he got out of the car and followed me tiredly over to the plane.

He was my best friend.

And I've never in my life yelled at anyone the way I yelled at Clarke, my best friend. Never.

Everything in me balked at it, but I hardened myself and continued to yell. I was close to tears, gritting my teeth.

It sounds heroic, but it wasn't at all.

It was just hard, and unbelievably wearing.

And sad, as well.

Is this yours? was Clarke's only response. He sounded tired. I nodded casually.

Flew this one a few years ago, he continued hesitantly, and I sensed that I was on the right track.

It still took a considerable amount of time, and I felt drained, all my powers of persuasion stretched to the limit, but finally, he climbed clumsily onto the wing and peered into the front cockpit. I'd thought this through very carefully. Very precisely. Every sentence.

C'mon, sit down, I coaxed. *Need your help.*

He didn't want to. At all. But I didn't let up.

I was stubborn. It wasn't easy for me.

A quarter of an hour later, he was sitting up front in the cockpit. There was no time to lose now. I twisted around and hastily closed the canopy. *Let's take a ride,* I yelled.

I knew perfectly well that Clarke was in no state to fly the thing, and I wasn't sure whether his licence was even still valid. It wasn't as though he had his documents with him, anyway. I also knew perfectly well that I wasn't a flight instructor, nor did I have any right to introduce him to this aircraft. I'd never flown the thing from behind before, and had only logged a few hours messing around in it since taking my rating. So if something went wrong, it would have cost me all my credit plus an expensive lawsuit abroad. I knew all that perfectly well.

But it was the only chance to help my friend.

The only chance. And I knew that too. Perfectly well.

And, much more importantly, I trusted him.

And then it happened.

Suddenly, Clarke shook off his lethargy.

I watched in interest as, slowly but with great control, he strapped himself in, put the headset on and flipped switches and levers.

It seemed to me as though his fingers were rushing ahead of his sorrow and stasis, attempting to escape them.

The starter purred to life; the propeller spun a few times, and the engine bucked awake, spitting a blue cloud of oil smoke.

A crackle through the headset alerted me to the fact that Clarke had switched on the avionics.

As though the last few months had simply been a dream.

I pressed the mic button. *Are you okay, buddy?* I asked cautiously. *Yes, of course, kid,* he replied slowly.

It was another decisive moment. I pressed the mic button. *Listen,* I began, *I'll do the radio work with ATC, not you, please, okay?*

After a long pause, he reluctantly muttered, *Yes, Sir.*

I couldn't believe it at first; could hardly get over my own surprise.

Tower frequency, please, I requested, and asked for taxi clearance. I received and acknowledged it immediately.

Not a peep from Clarke.

Your control, Sir, I said carefully over the intercom, and he immediately responded, *My control.*

He opened the throttle and removed the parking brake with a jerk. Working the brakes delicately, he taxied to takeoff position as though it was the simplest thing in the world.

I'd barely finished repeating, *Cleared for take-off*, when Clarke thrust the throttle quickly forward and sent the plane thundering over the concrete.

He took off, much faster than the minimum safety speed, and put up the gear.

No stunts, please, they know a rookie is flying this bird, I said hastily, to prevent him from throwing the T-28 into a steep climb across the threshold.

The only response I got was a short confirmatory double click through the headset.

Following a meticulous ascent, we made a textbook entry into the traffic circuit and said our farewells to air traffic control. Clarke was like a different person; concentrating entirely on the task at hand; flying with such focus and ease that I almost burst with joy behind him.

We spent almost two hours in the air above England. Clarke began to narrate, words spilling from him like water. He pointed out old, abandoned bomber airfields from the war; we plunged through the low cumulus clouds; and finally, playful yet perfectly calm, he showed me how to do a slow, perfect barrel roll in the T-28, then made me practice it until he was satisfied.

We touched down softly at North Weald at noon on a beautiful warm British July day. Once we had taxied out and were sitting in front of the hangar with the engine muttering, the intercom crackled to life again. *Your control, Sir,* said Clarke.

The spell was broken. I rejoiced quietly.

My control.

The engine shuddered to a standstill.

Clarke shook off his seatbelt and hopped down from the cockpit to the wing, just like the Clarke I used to know. Behind the hangar. Nobody had noticed a thing.

Barely a week later - I was back home by then - Clarke's friend rang me from the airfield. He told me that Clarke had turned up again three days ago and driven everyone absolutely mad as he attempted to resurrect his Hurricane, which was on the point of being mothballed. He also said that, to top it all, Clarke had nearly murdered the medical examiner when the man hesitated to give him his medical.

The old Clarke was back, clearly.

I was so delighted I could have danced. My plan - or rather, my instinct -had worked.

Clarke is flying again now - not only his Hurricane, but everything else he can get his hands on too. We write to each other. We call each other. Just like before. I went across to see him just a few weeks later.

We visited Will's grave. And went away together to tell old stories. As one does.

Six months later, he came to visit me in Germany.

He had to see me, he wrote.

He had to. He needed to tell me something very important, he wrote, at once both voluble and shy.

So we met at a pub, and, once we'd finished eating, he gazed at me thoughtfully for a long time.

Then he stood up solemnly and began to explain something - as though he wanted to give a speech that he'd spent a lot of time and energy preparing, but the actual act of doing so was almost beyond him.

He stumbled over his words for so long that I eventually waved him to a halt, shaking my head, deeply moved.

Finally, I stood up too and begged him to sit down again.

And then we both burst into tears.

Nobody saw us.

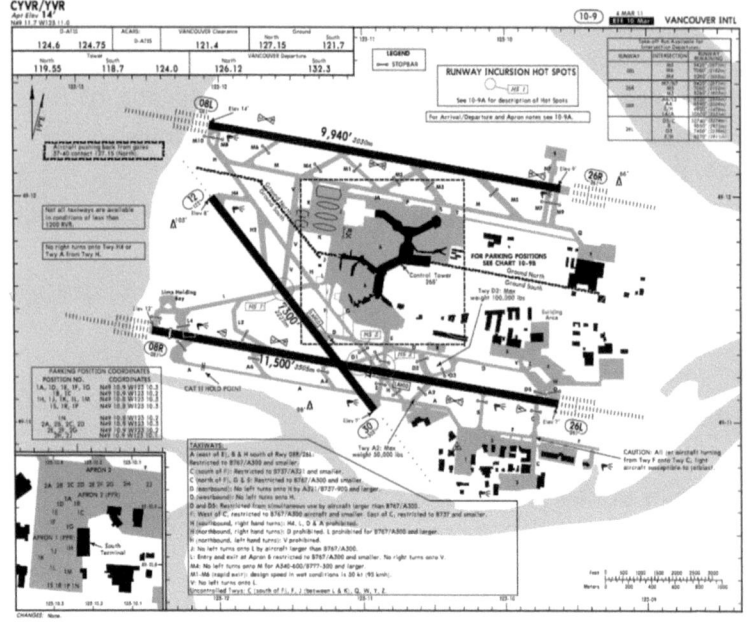

Air Canada Four-One-Seven

I had finished this book: all the stories were written and in place, the contents page was ready, the fore- and afterword were complete. And then, during the editing phase, I heard a story that gave me pause.

It was a recent recording of radio traffic between the tower in Vancouver and Flight Air Canada 417.

This conversation was recorded by the live feed of an ATC network, which makes radio traffic from various airports available online.

When I received the link to the story, I at first assumed it would be one of the usual funny stories where a pilot or controller goes rogue over the radio.
I put it on in the background. But in a flash, right after the initial call, something caught my attention.
Something was different. A mysterious sensation crept over me.

And it truly was something different. What I heard moved me very deeply. I listened to the recording a few times in a row. Nothing changed; I was still deeply affected.

I know how quickly these kinds of incidents surface and then vanish again online, so I decided to transcribe the conversation and preserve the story. Because I believe it's not something that will happen again. And it was immediately clear to me that this story needed to be a part of my book. It had to.

Some important background information: the text is an unabridged original transcript of the radio traffic between the Vancouver tower and Flight Air Canada 417.
I have changed the flight numbers and names. I've also attempted to describe each person's characteristic way of speaking with reference to their voices.

A little later, it came out that this radio conversation had largely taken place on a separate frequency once the plane had already landed. My research also confirmed that flight safety at Vancouver Airport and on Flight AC417 was not compromised at any point.
Both the courage of the controller, who kept trying to maintain

his coolness and composure despite the intense strain in his voice, and the kindness, empathy and openness of the cockpit crew on Flight AC417 moved me deeply.

Key:
TWR (tower)
Voice of the air traffic controller from the Vancouver tower
AC417 (Air Canada 417)
Voice(s) of the cockpit crew of Flight Air Canada 417
ROUGE349 (Air Canada Rouge)
Another approaching plane in the controller's sector

AC417 Tower, AC417, we are outside DAWG.

TWR (*very routined*): AC417, thank you, 08L, altimeter 2982, you're number one.

AC417 Roger, number one, AC417.

TWR AC417 you are cleared to land, runway 08L.

AC417 Cleared to land, 08L, AC417.

TWR AC417 exit next on the high speed, stay with me, what's your gate number?

AC417 We're not sure yet, but... probably Charlie five-one.

TWR Roger

(*short break*)

ROUGE349 ROUGE349 is with you, over...just about seven out.

TWR ROUGE 349, Tower, altimeter 2982, cleared to land, runway 08L

ROUGE349: 2982, cleared to land, runway 08L, tree-four-niner.

TWR (*a bit strained*) AC417, taxi Mike-Juliet, and Juliet-

Charlie.

AC417 Roger, AC417

TWR AC417, and...aaahm (*break*) my girlfriend is on that plane and I was gonna propose to her while you were in the air but I chickened out.

AC417 (*a bit John Wayne-like*) Come ooon! That's baaad, that's really bad.

Give us her name and we're gonna tell her that.

TWR Well, can I... (*short break*) is it too late?

AC417 Not too late. Not too late for anything! Do you know, where she's sitting?

TWR I think she's twentyfive-Charlie, her name ist Jennifer Rivers.

AC417 (*drawled*): Yeaaaaah. Let's see how we can do this. Stand by.

(*break*)

AC417 Just give me the seat number again and just double check her name, I'm gonna bring her up to the flight deck.

TWR (*a bit strained again*) Seat number is twentyfive-Charlie. And her name is Jennifer Rivers.

AC417 OK, stand by.

(*long break*)

AC417 You have a choice. We can put you on the microphone in front oft he whole airplane, or she can come to the flightdeck. It's your call.

TWR (*fast*) Well, put me in front of everybody.

AC417 All right.

(*long break*)

AC417 Ooookay, my friend, you are on the whole airplane, so go ahead and do your thing.

TWR (*forcing himself to speak calmly*) Good evening, ladies and gentleman, I'm your air traffic controller speaking to you from the control tower here in Vancover airport. I hope all of you have enjoyed your flight this evening with Air Canada from Montreal and I welcome all of you in Vancouver.

The reason I am speaking to you is because there is a very special lady on your flight this evening. Her name is Jennifer Rivers.

(*short break*)

TWR Jennifer, can you raise your hand, please? Way up, so everyone can see.

(*short break*)

TWR (*trying hard to sound calm*) Jennifer, I am crazy in love with you, can't imagine my life without you. You can't see me right now but I am down on my knee, I have a ring in my hand.

Jennifer, will you make me the happiest man in the world and be my wife?

(*break*)

AC417 (*very impressed!*) Everybody is jumping up and down and she said YES. I can hear it all the way back here.

(*break*)

AC417 I'll try to get her up in a minute.

TWR Thanks.

AC417 That was nicely done, by the way.

Very very nice.

AC417 (*very smooth*) And the whole airplane is shaking.

AC417 And she said YES. It's confirmed by the purser, my friend. I'll have her brought up to he flight deck, give me a second.

TWR (*absolutely relieved*) Hey thanks. I appreciate it!

AC417 Any time.

TWR AC417?

AC417 Go ahead.

TWR I'm just gonna be going off the frequency so I'll meet her at the luggage area.

AC417 OK, aaah, sure, if that's what works for you. No problem and all the best to you.

TWR All right, thank you very much.

And that's the end of the recording.

Perhaps some readers may find this incident and this story somewhat over-the-top or even out of place here. And maybe they're right. But this story moved me deeply and made it clear to me that - thankfully - I'm not the only totally romantic pilot in the world. And I'm grateful for that.

To the happy couple: fly high! I wish you every happiness, contentment and blessing.

If anyone had told me back then that one day I'd give up flying, I'd have called them crazy. All of them.

After all, no bird was hot enough back then.
Every flight was too short.
Every aerobatics programme ended too quickly.

After my very first boyhood flight, I devoured everything that had to do with aviation. I assembled model aircraft like crazy; I spend endless hours standing at airfield fences, to which I drove miles by bike only to see the jets or helicopters rushing over me; steadily drank in literature and films about aviation. I always dreamed of learning to fly myself; dreamed myself into countless different aircraft.
During the time of my flying, I was able to achieve an

incredible amount. Much more than I ever dreamed of back then.
More percisely: Much, much more.

Many flight hours in many different aircraft from many different places; from so many airfields; in the most bizarre locations.
An impossible number of experiences.

I flew slowly - and very, very quickly.
I flew breathtakingly low - and very, very high.
Very loud and very soft.
I flew upside down; I flew in open cockpits and cramped up in narrow turrets.
I flew close to the clouds and far up above the world.
I made many good friends.
So much enthusiasm, so many crazy schemes, so much advice.
In so many different countries.
I met veterans who told me about their flying days and their friends with tears in their eyes.
I visited sites that had stories to tell about the bygone days of aviation and of experiences that we are spared today.
I met people who put their energy and enthusiasm into maintaining aircraft, into keeping them in the sky.
And I was able to fly with some of them.

One day, I realised I had everything that had once seemed unattainable.
And at some point, I began flying less.
Not deliberately.

It felt perfectly normal.

Eventually, I was no longer flying enough hours to keep my licence.
So I gave it up.
It sounds crazy, I know.

But I had had the gift, the indescribable happiness, of seeing the world from up there.

And I felt that was enough.

For more than one lifetime.

First and foremost, I owe the most thanks to my wife, who encouraged me to keep working on this book and who also supported me with her wise advice and skilful editing.
I have to thank *Thea Bradbury* for this very attentive and wonderful translation. Without her dedicated and sensitive treatment this book would not have been published in such a way.

Thanks to *Thomas Lange*, who encouraged me to keep writing from very early on.
Thank you to Christoph *Charlie Zulu* Zischek for the blurb.
And thank you to everybody who helped to shape this book, whether directly or indirectly.
I've undoubtedly forgotten someone - please forgive me.

The names are presented in alphabetical order.

à persona:

Jan Ahlers, Peter `Pete´ Allen, Siegfried `Siggi´ Angerer,
Wilfried Birkholz, Nicholas `Nick´ Bradbury, Thea Bradbury,
Cornelius Braun, Thomas `Tom´ Bode, Phillipp `Brommel´
Brombach, Ferdy Doernberg, Walter u. Tony Eichhorn, Richard
M. `Gitts´ Gittins (†), Geoff Goodall, Mark Hannah (†), Dirk
Heuer, Christian `Schorsch´ Homuth, Christoph `Jeany´ Jehn,
Klaus `Kellogs´ Kellermeier, Ulf Kleinau, Harald `Harry´ Krainz,
E.-D. `Balou´ Köster, Roland und Thomas Lange, Steffen
Leuer, Rainer `Spooky´ Luff, Klaus Marzina, Fee und Günther
Meidenbauer, Dr. Peter Müller (†), Hilmar Nicklaus (†), Frank
Paul, Klaus `Joe´ Plaza, Bernd Pfähler, Ludwig `Louis´ Prüß,
Anders K. Saether, Reinhardt Schramme, Selma und Jürgen
(†) Schlee, Gerd `Schimi´ Schimanski, Tom Schulz, Jane
Simmonds, RAF Air Marshall (ret.) Clifford R. Spink, Friedhelm
Stahlhut, Hermann Steckhan (†), Theo Schuhmacher, Heribert
Schwab, K.- H. Telkemeier (†), Jürgen und Hanne Wilhelm,
Werner Vogt, Kurt `Automatic´ Vockel, Kermit Weeks, Björn
`Scope´ Wehrmacher, Hans Wiesman, Uwe Wiesner, Günter
Witting (†), Charles `Chuck´ Yeager, Britt Zahn, Thilo von Zahn,
Christa und Helmut Zischek sowie Christoph `Charlie-Zulu´
Zischek.

And to everyone else who has been a part of my journey:

Germany:
- Luftsportverein Bückeburg Weinberg
  (ex- Segelflugverein Schaumburg) `Weinberg Sierra`
- 307. Squadron
- Aero-Club Minden (EDVY)
- Sportfluggruppe Nordholz (ETMN)
- ex- MfG 2 `Vikings` Eggebek (ETME)
- LTG 63 (ETNH)
- LTG 62 (ETNW)
- IHAS (ex- Heeresfliegerwaffenschule I / ETHB)
- JG 71 `Richthofen` (ETNT)
- ex- AG-51 (EDTG)
- RK-Flugdienst (EDHE)
- Messerschmitt-Stiftung (ETSI)
- Hubschraubermuseum Bückeburg
- Luftwaffenmuseum Gatow (ex- EDBG)
- RAF Gütersloh: Royal Air Cadets, No. 3 Sqdr. & No. 4 Sqdr.
  (ETUO)

Austria:
- The Flying Bulls - Hangar 7 (LOWS)

Danmark:
- Danmarks Flymuseum Stauning, DK
- Herning Svæveflyveklub (EKHG)

The Netherlands:
- The Royal Netherlands Air Force Historical Flight Foundation
  (ex- Duke Of Brabant Air Force / EHGR)

Scandinavia:
- ex- Scandinavian Historic Flight (ENGM)

Poland:
- Aeroklub Leszczynski (EPLS)

Hungary:
- Szombathely Aerodrome (LHSY)

France:
- Aéroclub du Pays d' Ancenis (LFFI)
- Aeròdrom de la Cerdanya (LECD)
- La Fertè-Alais (LFFQ)
- Musée Du Débarquement Utah Beach
  (Sainte Marie Du Mont / FR)

Great Britain:
- Battle Of Britain Memorial Flight / RAF Conningsby (EGXC)
- The Fighter Collection (EGSU)
- B-17 Preservation Ltd. (EGSU)
- The Catalina Society (EGSU)
- Imperial War Museum (EGSU)
- The Kent Battle Of Britain Museum, Hawkinge / UK
- Old Flying Machine Company (EGSU)
- North Weald Airfield Museum (EGSX)
- former RAF Horsham St. Faith (EGSH)

- Spitfire and Hurricane Memorial Museum (EGMH)

United States Of America:
- Collings Foundation, Staw / CA, U.S.A.
- Fantasie Of Flight, Polk City / FL, U.S.A.
- Smithonian´s National Air And Space Museum Washington /
  DC, U.S.A.
- Commemorate Air Force / Midland TX, U.S.A.
- Planes Of Fame Museum / Chino CA, U.S.A.
- A-26K Special Kay - Team / Fort Worth TX, U.S.A.

Jordania:
- The Royal Jordanian Falcons (OJMF)